BREAST STORIES

MAHASWETA DEVI

Translated with introductory essays by
GAYATRI CHAKRAVORTY SPIVAK

CALCUTTA 1997

Cover image: Chittrovanu Mazumdar
Cover design: Naveen Kishore

ISBN 81 7046 140 5

The publishers gratefully acknowledge Routledge, New York, for permission to reprint the following—'Draupadi: Translator's Foreword'; 'Draupadi'; 'Breast-Giver'; and the essay entitled '"Breast-Giver": For Author, Reader . . . ' which is an adapted, lightly edited version of an earlier essay which, along with the other pieces, previously appeared in *In Other Worlds: Essays in Cultural Politics*, by Gayatri Chakravorty Spivak (Methuen, New York, 1987).

Published by Naveen Kishore,
Seagull Books Private Limited
26 Circus Avenue, Calcutta 700 017, India

Printed in India by Laurens & Co,
9 Crooked Lane, Calcutta 700 069

The Selected Works of Mahasweta Devi

Mahasweta Devi (b. 1926) is one of our foremost literary personalities, a prolific and best-selling author in Bengali of short fiction and novels; a deeply political social activist who has been working with and for tribals and marginalized communities like the landless labourers of eastern India for years; the editor of a quarterly, *Bortika*, in which the tribals and marginalized peoples themselves document grassroot level issues and trends; and a socio-political commentator whose articles have appeared regularly in the *Economic and Political Weekly*, *Frontier* and other journals.

Mahasweta Devi has made important contributions to literary and cultural studies in this country. Her empirical research into oral history as it lives in the cultures and memories of tribal communities was a first of its kind. Her powerful, haunting tales of exploitation and struggle have been seen as rich sites of feminist discourse by leading scholars. Her innovative use of language has expanded the conventional borders of Bengali literary expression. Standing as she does at the intersection of vital contemporary questions of politics, gender and class, she is a significant figure in the field of socially committed literature.

Recognizing this, we have conceived a publishing programme which encompasses a representational look at the complete Mahasweta: her novels, her short fiction, her children's stories, her plays, her activist prose writings. The series is an attempt to introduce her impressive body of work to a readership beyond Bengal; it is also an overdue recognition of the importance of her contribution to the literary and cultural history of our country.

The Selected Works of Mahasweta Devi

Mother of 1084
A Novel.Translated and introduced by
Samik Bandyopadhyay.

Breast Stories: Draupadi, Breast-Giver, Choli ke Pichhe
Translated with introductory essays by
Gayatri Chakravorty Spivak.

Five Plays: Mother of 1084, Aajir, Urvashi and Johnny, Bayen, Water
Adapted from her fiction by the author.
Translated and introduced by
Samik Bandyopadhyay.

Rudali: From Fiction to Performance
This volume consists of the story by Mahasweta Devi
and the play by Usha Ganguli.
Translated and introduced by Anjum Katyal.

The Activist Writings of Mahasweta Devi
A collection of articles published in
Economic and Political Weekly, Frontier, and other journals.
Introduced and translated by Maitreya Ghatak.

CONTENTS

introduction

gayatri chakravorty spivak

THIS INTRODUCTION WAS to have been called The Breast Trilogy. Mahasweta Devi is writing another story about the breast.Let us look forward to The Breast Series.

The breast is not a symbol in these stories. In 'Draupadi', what is represented is an erotic object transformed into an object of torture and revenge where the line between (hetero)sexuality and gender violence begins to waver. In 'Breast-Giver,' it is a survival object transformed into a commodity, making visible the indeterminacy between filial piety and gender violence, between house and temple, between domination and exploitation. Devi's mature fiction never romanticizes the socio-libidinal relationship between the sexes. In 'Behind the Bodice,' she bitterly decries the supposed 'normality' of sexuality as male violence.[1] In the eyes of the Caretaker, it is just that

Gangor's breasts have been destroyed. If 'the girl doesn't understand the police are men too, they will craze if you tease them'. In the process Mahasweta fixes her glance at art, 'popular' and 'high,'pulp filmmaker and archivalist photographer. The point is not just aesthetics and politics, but aesthetics and ethics, archivization and responsibility.

The breast is what the stories have in common. What they don't share is shown by the staging of the names of the three protagonists: Dopdi, Jashoda, Gangor; in 'Draupadi,' 'Breast-Giver,' 'Behind the Bodice.'

'Breast-Giver' is the story that builds itself on the cruel ironies of caste, class, patriarchy. Devi keeps Jashoda's name unchanged from the Sanskrit scriptural form. Although the orthodox Hindu middle class nominally reveres the brahmin, the prerogatives of economic class are in fact much more real for it. The underclass 'Hindu female' ('Breast-Giver'), as long as she credits Hindu maternalism and family values, is unable to save herself. Even in her lonely death, she remains 'Jashoda *Devi*'—literally, the goddess Jashoda, honorary goddess by caste.

It is the Aboriginal Dopdi and the migrant proletarian Gangor who are the subjects of resistant rage.[2] Their names bear the mark of their distance from the top: the Aboriginal's immediate ('Dopdi' although she was named Draupadi by her brahmin mistress) and the Dalit's historical: Gangor from Ganagauri, 'corrupt' through usage.

Here, too, there is a difference. We are as sure of the derivation of Dopdi from Draupadi as we are of the author's hardly implicit point of view. The story of

Draupadi, the narrative efficient cause of the battle of the great epic *Mahabharata*, is wellknown in India. God had prevented male lust from unclothing her. And she had had five husbands. This Dopdi, gang-raped by police, refuses to be clothed by men in office.

(The mythic Jashoda's story is also wellknown. She is the foster-mother of Krishna, in Hindu Bengal a famous erotic god; in his role as strategist and adviser, it is he who saves Draupadi from dishonour.)

Although the power of Gangor's resistance and rage is, if anything, worked out more explicitly than Dopdi's —Gangor explicitly accuses the police—the staging of the provenance of her name is interestingly obscure. 'Ganagauri' as the origin of 'Gangor' is a bit of documentation offered by the most problematic character in 'Behind the Bodice,' Shital Mallya, the 'new' Indian woman, the mountain-climbing individualist in a liberated marriage, official interpreter for 'The Festival of India' (an elaborate museumized international self-representation of Indian 'culture' as arrested pre-capitalist tradition of folk-artisanal ethnic simplicity). The reader cannot be sure if Shital is right or wrong about this. It is, however, quite certain that her explanation, given in tones of contempt to an 'uncultured' Indian, is ridiculously wrong. The name Ganagauri has nothing to do with the river Ganga.

This is a new object of critique for Mahasweta: 'Indian intellectuals not knowing a single Indian language meet in a closed *seminar* in the capital city and make the[ir] wise decision known:' the custodians of Indian culture. Mahasweta is altogether uninterested in fragmenting India along language lines. Her extraordinary command of Dalit North Indian heteroglossia is proof of how far she has expanded her own Bengali language base.[3] She is, however, equally uninterested in handing over India's heterogeneity to this new consumerist class, politically correct by international coding, full of a class contempt that is either open, or disguised by impersonal benevolence.

When in 1981, I had suggested that the expert on Third World resistant literature nourished by First World civil societies had something like a relationship with the police chief in 'Draupadi,' diasporic commentators had been displeased. Perhaps I had stated my case too strongly. In 'Behind the Bodice,' Mahasweta refines the point. Even when the expert is 'good,' the cultural worker as such is not by that fact resistant. (By contrast, in the figure of the 106-year old freedom fighter, Mahasweta lodges an affectionate aside for those who see every contemporary event as 'colonial discourse.') 'There is no *non-issue* behind the bodice, there is a rape of the people behind it, Upin would have known if he had wanted to, could have known'.

'Rape of the people'—ganadharshan. Here the name Ganagauri has quite another resonance. For 'gana' is, ot course, 'demos,'—the people—as in 'democracy'—ganatantra. Behind the bodice is a rape of the people. Here the breast becomes a concept-metaphor (rather than a symbol) of police violence in the democratic state. In a comparable though not identical way, Buchi Emecheta will not let the rape of Ayoko 'stand for' collaborative colonial exploitation in *The Rape of Shavi.*

It is precisely the figure that I am loosely calling the 'expert' that Devi has fine-tuned and diversified. The readership of these Englished stories (though not necessarily of all her work) will contain many such figures. Puran in 'Pterodactyl, Puran Sahay, and Pirtha' writes *two* reports, one suppressed in the imagination, and leaves the valley, forever marked in his being. Upin, too, is marked by Gangor's case and rage; and dies, either by chance brought on by confusion, or by choice.

Here a word on nature, artifice, or prosthesis may be appropriate.

I have often been critical of the French historian Michel Foucault in the context of the critique of imperialism. But one lesson superficial Enlightenment-merchants would do well to learn from him: that resistance inscribes itself in polarities available in the discursive formation. 'Power' *is* nothing if not opposed to what it is not, by those rules of the discursive formation that are not only larger than personal good- or ill-will, but indeed make the latters' forms of expression concretely possible.

Moving by this Foucauldian intuition we might say that academic US feminism names social-constructionism as 'anti-essentialism,' and polarizes it against 'nature' because, briefly, this is how their discursive formation de-fangs Marxist-materialist radicalism. I therefore point out that we translate as 'nature' *two* Bengali words—shobhab (Sansk. *swabhava*) and prakriti—and will continue to do so because they relate to an equally vague split in the English word: characteristic behavior on the one hand, and that part of the animate universe which is taken to be without reasonable consciousness, on the other. A contrast derived from this split is used by Marx to explain 'value:' a contrast between the 'raw' (material=nature) and the cooked (fabricated=commodity, the German

Fabrik being, also, factory).[4] I have pointed elsewhere at the meretricious political results of understanding 'nature' in Bengali usage as mere 'essentialism' without attention to the general framework of the argument.[5] Here let me point out that the same sort of problem might arise from an impatient or careless reading of Upin's *anagnorisis*: 'Gangor's developed breasts are natural, not manufactured. Why did he first think they were the object of photography? Why did it seem that that chest was endangered?".

The first mistake would, of course, be the intentional fallacy: to mistake the staging of a character's realization in a moment of anguish as the author's own Luddite (or 'essentialist') tendencies. But the second mistake, which takes into account that the author-text opposition might itself be interested, is more dangerous. It spells the rejection of resistant polarizations by assigning master-meanings to single English words, by treating polarizations within the various histories of English as 'natural.'

Upin is not shown to be engaged in a celebration of the 'natural'. His realization is that he had made a mistake in assuming that the part object ('that chest') is no more than the object of photography as prosthesis for permanence, a species of silicone implant, as it were. There is a moment, earlier, when even the superficial contrast is undermined—even stone sculpture, *as sculpture,* erodes, for erosion is 'natural'. But is it, with chemical pollution in the air? And how chemical is photography? The thoughtful reader enters a labyrinth here that can deroute Plato's critique of writing as *hypermnesis* or 'memory implant' and accomodate Marx's critique of mistaking the social (rational, abstract average, spectral) *relationship* between human beings as the relationship between things. To preserve the breast as aesthetic *object* by photography or implant is to overlook its value-coding within patriarchal social relationship: it is 'natural' that men should be men. It is therefore 'natural' that women should be modest, and not provoke, by making the living breast dance.

It is my misfortune that I read literature as teaching texts. Therefore, helped by the arrangement of Mahasweta's story, I must go from this point to another. Upin made Gangor self-conscious about the unique beauty of her breasts, without any thought of the social repercussions. His political correctness ended with personally not lusting after Gangor's breasts: 'Learn to praise and respect a beautiful thing,' he chides. I cannot not read this as a literary representation of anchorless 'consciousness-raising' without shouldering any responsibility for infrastructural implementation. Those who already know what I am describing will need no examples. Those who do not will learn nothing from the only example I will cite here: credit-baiting through women's 'micro-enterprise' while removing infrastructural supports in the society at large: rape of the people. There is no figure of violence in such a global case to make the disaster immediately visible. And the most active collaborators, to keep the violence invisible by ignorance or design, are the 'New Women' of the South, 'cultural interpreters,' hybridists or popular culturists when necessary, environmentalists when possible, quite like Shital Mallya or Gayatri Spivak. Does Mahasweta do them an injustice? No doubt. Historical responsibility is asymmetrical. The rich and the poor are not equally free to sleep under the bridges of Paris.

We hope Mahasweta Devi will continue to write her 'breast' stories, for the breast is indeed a powerful part object, permitting the violent coming-into-being of the human, on the uncertain cusp of nature and culture. In 1986, writing on 'Breast-giver,' I had invoked Lacan. I did not then know of a generally unacknowledged debt to Melanie Klein.[6]

Klein's work has been almost fully appropriated by the patriarchal maternalist establishment of British Kleinian psychoanalysis. If, however, Klein is read without fear of that authoritative restricted interpretation, the following summary can be made:

The infant has one object with which to begin to construct the systems of truth (meaning) and goodness (responsibility) which will make it human. This object is its source of nourishment, deprivation, and sensuality—usually the breast. At weaning and before, the breast—and, secondarily, other part objects—become 'symbolized' and recognized as whole persons. Our sense of what it means to be human is played out in scenarios of guilt and reparation where the object is the primary part object incessantly transmogrified into people and other collectivities.

To tie human subject formation to Oedipus was to tie it to the patriarchal nuclear family. To make it depend upon the primary part object (overwhelmingly still the breast) as chief instrument for the production of truth and lie (signification) and of good and evil (responsibility) is to free it from that historical bondage.

Behind the bodice is therefore the long-ago part object that plays in the constant dynamic of the construction of whole persons. We see Gangor first with her breast carelessly lodged in the child's mouth. And it is the child, crying, that brings Upin's guilt home to him. These are not logical but figural connections. This is not maternalism but a reminder of the line from the breast as part-object to the 'whole person' who is the impossible presupposition of all ethical action. To 'save' the part object (save that chest, 'save the breast') as art object (is Mahasweta thinking of 'save the dance not the dancer?'—the slogan that led to the simultaneous establishment of kalakshetras and the Indian classical dance forms as such; and the devastation of devadasis into whores' colonies?) is to shortcircuit that presupposition. By the time Upin knows this, the breasts are destroyed and Gangor, the agent of resistant rage, finds him guilty. If theory is judged in its setting to work, here is a fable of justice. Mary Oraon, technically a murderer, runs along the railroad track toward an open future.[7] Upin Puri, technically innocent but judged by his victim, encounters his sentence upon the tracks. Senanayak ('Draupadi') had only been afraid. If one wishes to construct a pattern in Devi's breast-fiction or woman-fiction, this may be one.

In the current global conjuncture, then, behind the bodice is the rape of the people: choli ke pichhe ganadharshan. The archivist could not understand it,. and died in the understanding. Let us call it archive-fever.[8]

October 1996, Calcutta GCS

Notes

1. The translator has published separate essays on 'Draupadi' and 'Breast-Giver,' which are reproduced here from Spivak, *In Other Worlds: Essays in Cultural Politics* (New York and London: Methuen, 1987) on pgs. 1 and 76 respectively. This

essay attends more particularly to 'Behind the Bodice.'

2. Readers who think of 'India' or 'Woman' as monolithic have complained that Mahasweta's depiction of them is not uniformly upbeat. I hope this invocation of heterogeneity will answer them.

3. In fact, the Dalit 'national' language is generally a combination of dialectal variants of the local language, of Hindi, the 'official' national language, and phonotypes from the lexicalized indigenous English of India. It is a pity that translation cannot keep track of Devi's movement from standard Bengali to varieties of local dialects, not only the one I have just described.

4. Karl Marx, *Capital: a Critique of Political Economy,* tr. Ben Fowkes (New York: Vintage, 1976–81), p. 129f.

5. Spivak, 'Diasporas Old and New: Women in a Transnational World,' *Textual Practice* 10(2) (1996), p. 245–260, n 9.

6. For Lacan's reading of Klein, consult Shuan-hung Wu, Department of English, Columbia University; for Derrida's reading, see Spivak, tr. *Of Grammatology* (Baltimore: Johns Hopkins Univ. Press, 1976), p.88; for Deleuze and Guattari, see Robert Hurley et. al., tr. *Anti-Oedipus: Capitalism and Schizophrenia* (Minneapolis: Univ. of Minnesota Press, 1977), p.324 and *passim.* These writers often miss Klein's boldness because of their less practical, less womanist relationship to the importance of the family in the bag of tricks that society gives us to make sense of our lives and within which we play out our sense of human responsibility.

7. Devi, 'The Hunt' in *Imaginary Maps,* tr. Spivak (Calcutta: Thema, 1993) p.1.

8. Jacques Derrida, 'Archive-Fever,' *Diacritics* 25 (Summer 1995), p. 9–63. Why should we listen to Derrida, Foucault, Klein? Because they have seen 'only the Enlightenment' from close up. We cannot and must not do without the fruits of the Enlightenment. The point is to use them from below. But that is another story.

draupadi
translator's foreword[1]

I TRANSLATED THIS BENGALI SHORT STORY into English as much for the sake of its villain, Senanayak, as for its title character, Draupadi (or Dopdi). Because in Senanayak I find the closest approximation to the First-World scholar in search of the Third World, I shall speak of him first.

On the level of the plot, Senanayak is the army officer who captures and degrades Draupadi. I will not go so far as to suggest that, in practice, the instruments of First-World life and investigation are complicit with such captures and such a degradation.[2] The approximation I notice relates to the author's careful presentation of Senanayak as a pluralist aesthete. In *theory*, Senanayak can identify with the enemy. But pluralist aesthetes of the First World are, willy-nilly, participants in the production of an exploitative society. Hence in *practice*, Senanayak must destroy the enemy, the menacing other. He follows the necessities and contingencies of what he sees as his historical moment. There is a convenient colloquial name for that as well: pragmatism. Thus his emotions at Dopdi's capture are mixed: sorrow (theory) and joy (practice). Correspondingly, we grieve for our Third-World sisters; we grieve and rejoice that they must lose themselves and become as much like us as possible in order to be 'free'; we congratulate ourselves on our specialists' knowledge of them. Indeed, like ours, Senanayak's project is interpretive: he looks to decipher Draupadi's song. For both sides of the rift within himself, he finds analogies in Western literature: Hochhuth's *The Deputy*, David Morell's *First Blood*. He will shed his guilt when the time comes. His self-image for that uncertain future is Prospero.

I have suggested elsewhere that, when we wander out of our own academic and First-World enclosure, we share something like a relationship with Senanayak's doublethink.[3] When we speak for ourselves, we urge with conviction: the personal is also political. For the rest of the world's women, the sense of whose personal micrology is difficult (though not impossible) for us to acquire, we fall back on a colonialist theory of most efficient information retrieval. We will not be able to speak to the women out there if we depend completely on conferences and anthologies by Western-trained informants. As I see their photographs in women's-studies journals or on book jackets—indeed, as I look in the glass—it is Senanayak with his anti-Fascist paperbacks that I behold. In inextricably mingling historico-political specificity with the sexual differential in a literary discourse, Mahasweta Devi invites us to begin effacing that image.

My approach to the story has been influenced by 'deconstructive practice'. I clearly share an unease that would declare avant-garde theories of interpretation too elitist to cope with revolutionary feminist material. How, then, has the practice of deconstruction been helpful in this context?

The aspect of deconstructive practice that is best known in the United States is its tendency toward infinite regression. The aspect that interests me most is, however, the recognition, within deconstructive practice, of provisional and intractable starting points in any investigative effort; its disclosure of complicities where a will to knowledge would create oppositions; its insistence that in disclosing complexities the critic-as-subject is herself complicit with the object of her critique; its emphasis upon 'history' and upon the ethico-political as the 'trace' of that complicity—the proof that we do not inhabit a clearly defined critical space free of such traces; and, finally, the acknowledgment that its own discourse can never be adequate to its example.[4] This is clearly not the place to elaborate each item upon this list. I should, however, point out that in my introductory paragraphs I have already situated the figure of Senanayak in terms of our own patterns of complicity. In what follows, the relationship between the tribal and classical characters of Draupadi, the status of Draupadi at the end of the story, and the reading of Senanayak's proper name might be seen as produced by the reading practice I have described. The complicity of law and transgression and the class deconstruction of the 'gentlemen revolutionaries,' although seemingly minor points in the interpretation of the story as such, take on greater importance in a political context.

I cannot take this discussion of deconstruction far enough to show how Dopdi's song, incomprehensible yet trivial (it is in fact about beans of different colours), and ex-orbitant to the story, marks the place of that other that can be neither excluded nor recuperated.[5]

'Draupadi' first appeared in *Agnigarbha* ('Womb of Fire'), a collection of loosely connected, short political narratives. As Mahasweta points out in her introduction to the collection, 'Life is not mathematics and the human being is not made for the sake of politics. I want a change in the present social system and do not believe in mere party politics.'[6]

Mahasweta is a middle-class Bengali activist writer and interventionist journalist with a long commitment to the left. She has a master's degree in English from Santiniketan, the famous experimental university established by Rabindranath Tagore. Her reputation as a novelist was already well established when, in the late '70s, she published *Hajar Churashir Ma* ('Mother of 1084'). This novel remains within the dominant psychological idiom of the Bengali fiction of its time.[7] Yet in *Aranyer Adhikar* ('The Rights (or Occupation) of the Forest'), a serially published novel she was writing almost at the same time, a significant change is noticeable. It is a meticulously researched historical novel about the Munda Insurrection of 1899-1900. Here Mahasweta begins putting together a prose that is a collage of literary Bengali, bureaucratic Bengali, tribal Bengali, and the languages of the tribals.

Since the Bengali script is illegible except to the approximately twenty-five percent literate of the about ninety million speakers of Bengali, a large number of whom live in Bangladesh rather than in West Bengal,[8] her 'Indian' reception is also in translation, in various languages of the subcontinent and in English. Briefly, that reception can be described as a general recognition of excellence; scepticism regarding the content on the part of the bourgeois readership; some accusations of extremism from the electoral Left; and admiration and a sense of solidarity on the part of the nonelectoral Left. Any extended reception study would consider that West Bengal has had a largely uninterrupted Left-Front government of the united electoral Communist parties since 1967. Here suffice it to say that Mahasweta is certainly one of the most important writers writing in India today.

Any sense of Bengal as a 'nation' is governed by the putative identity of the Bengali language.[9] (Meanwhile, Bengalis dispute if the purest Bengali is that of Nabadwip or South Calcutta, and many of the twenty-odd developed dialects are incomprehensible to the 'general speaker.') In 1947, on the eve of its departure from India, the British government divided Bengal into West Bengal, which remained a part of India, and East Pakistan. Punjab was similarly divided into East Punjab (India) and West Pakistan. The two parts of Pakistan did not share ethnic or linguistic ties and were separated by nearly eleven hundred miles. The division was made on the grounds of the concentration of Muslims in these two parts of the subcontinent. Yet the Punjabi Muslims felt themselves to be more 'Arab' because they lived in the area where the first Muslim emperors of India had settled nearly seven hundred years ago and also because of their proximity to West Asia (the Middle East). The Bengali Muslims—no doubt in a class-differentiated way —felt themselves constituted by the culture of Bengal.

Bengal has had a strong presence of leftist intellectualism and struggle since the middle of the last century, before, in fact, the word 'Left' entered our political shorthand.[10] As such, it is a source of considerable political irritation to the central government of India (The individual state governments have a good deal more autonomy under the Indian constitution than is the case in the US.) Although officially India was, until recently, a Socialist state with a mixed economy, historically it has reflected a spectrum of the Right, from military dictatorship to nationalist class benevolence. The word 'democracy' becomes highly interpretable in the context of a largely illiterate, multilingual, heterogeneous, and unpoliticized electorate.

In the spring of 1967, there was a successful peasant rebellion in the Naxalbari area of the northern part of West Bengal. According to Marcus Franda, 'unlike most other areas of West Bengal, where peasant movements are led almost solely by middle-class leadership from Calcutta, Naxalbari has spawned an indigenous agrarian reform leadership led by the lower classes' including tribal cultivators.[11] This peculiar coalition of peasant and intellectual sparked off a number of Naxalbaris all over India.[12] The target of these movements was the long-established oppression of the landless peasantry and itinerant farm worker, sustained through an unofficial government-landlord collusion that too easily circumvented the law. Indeed, one might say that legislation seemed to have an eye to its own future circumvention.

It is worth remarking that this coalition of peasant and intellectual—with long histories of apprenticeship precisely on the side of the intellectual—has been recuperated in the West by both ends of the polarity that constitutes a 'political spectrum.' Bernard-Henri Lévy, the ex-Maoist French 'New Philosopher,' has implicitly compared it to the May 1968 'revolution' in France, where the students joined the workers.[13] In France, however the student identity of the movement had remained clear, and the student leadership had not brought with it sustained efforts to undo the privilege of the intellectual. On the other hand, 'in much the same manner as many American college presidents have described the protest of American students, Indian political and social leaders have explained the Naxalites (supporters of Naxalbari) by referring to their sense of alienation and to the influence of writers like Marcuse and Sartre which has seemingly dominated the minds of young people throughout the world in the 1960s.'[14]

It is against such recuperations that I would submit what I have called the theme of class deconstruction with reference to the young gentlemen revolutionaries in 'Draupadi.' Senanayak remains fixed within his class origins, which are similar to those of the gentlemen revolutionaries. Correspondingly, he is contained and judged fully within Mahasweta's story; by contrast, the gentlemen revolutionaries remain latent, underground. Even their leader's voice is only heard formulaically within Draupadi's solitude. I should like to think that it is because they are so persistently engaged in undoing class containment and the opposition between reading (book learning) and doing—rather than keeping the two aesthetically forever separate—that they inhabit a world whose authority and outline no text—including Mahasweta's—can encompass.

In 1970, the implicit hostility between East and West Pakistan flamed into armed struggle. In 1971, at a crucial moment in the struggle, the armed forces of the government of India were deployed, seemingly because these were alliances between the Naxalites of West Bengal and the freedom fighters of East Bengal (now Bangladesh). 'If a guerrilla-style insurgency had persisted, there forces would undoubtedly have come to dominate the politics of the movement. It was this trend that the Indian authorities were determined to pre-empt by intervention.' Taking advantage of the general atmosphere of jubilation at the defeat of West Pakistan, India's 'principal national rival in South Asia'[15] (this was also the first time India had 'won a war' in its millennial history), the Indian Prime Minister was able to crack down with exceptional severity on the Naxalites, destroying the rebellious sections of the rural population, most significantly the tribals, as well. The year 1971 is thus a point of reference in Senanayak's career.

This is the setting of 'Draupadi.' The story is a moment caught between two deconstructive formulas: on the one hand, a law that is fabricated with a view to its own transgression, on the other, the undoing of the binary opposition between the intellectual and the rural struggles. In order to grasp the minutiae of their relationship and involvement, one must enter a historical micrology that no foreword can provide.

Draupadi is the name of the central character. She is introduced to the reader between two uniforms and between two versions of her name. Dopdi and Draupadi. It is either that as a tribal she cannot pronounce her own Sanskrit name Draupadi, or the tribalized form, Dopdi, is the proper name of the ancient Draupadi. She is on a list of wanted persons, yet her name is not on the list of appropriate names for the tribal women.

The ancient Draupadi is perhaps the most celebrated heroine of the Indian epic *Mahabharata*. The *Mahabharata* and the *Ramayana* are the cultural credentials of the so-called Aryan civilization of India. The tribes predate the Aryan invasion. They have no right to heroic Sanskrit names. Neither the interdiction nor the significance of the name, however, must be taken too seriously. For this pious, domesticated Hindu name was given Dopdi at birth by her mistress, in the usual mood of benevolence felt by the oppressor's wife toward the tribal bond servant. It is the killing of this mistress's husband that sets going the events of the story.

And yet on the level of the text, this elusive and fortuitous name does play a role. To speculate upon this role, we might consider the *Mahabharata* itself in its colonialist function in the interest of the so-called Aryan invaders of India. It is an accretive epic, where the 'sacred' geography of an ancient battle is slowly expanded by succeeding generations of poets so that the secular geography of the expanding Aryan colony can present itself as identical with it and thus justify itself.[16] The complexity of this vast and anonymous project makes it an incomparably more heterogeneous text than the *Ramayana*. Unlike the *Ramayana*, for example, the *Mahabharata* contains cases of various kinds of kinship structure and various styles of marriage. And in fact it is Draupadi who provides the only example of polyandry, not a common system of marriage in India. She is married to the five sons of the impotent Pandu. Within a patriarchal and patronymic context, she is exceptional, indeed 'singular' in the sense of odd, unpaired, uncoupled.[17] Her husbands, since they are husbands rather than lovers, are *legitimately pluralized.* No acknowledgment of paternity can secure the Name of the Father for the child of such a mother. Mahasweta's story questions this 'singularity' by placing Dopdi first in a comradely, activist, monogamous marriage and then in a situation of multiple rape.

In the epic, Draupadi's legitimized pluralization (as a wife among husbands), in singularity (as a possible mother or harlot) is used to demonstrate male glory. She provides the occasion for a violent transaction between men, the efficient cause of the crucial battle. Her eldest husband is about to lose her by default in a game of dice. He had staked all he owned, and 'Draupadi belongs within that all' (*Mahabharata* 65:32). Her strange civil status seems to offer grounds for her predicament as well. 'The Scriptures prescribed one husband for a woman; Draupadi is dependent on many husbands; therefore she can be designated a prostitute. There is nothing improper in bringing her, clothed or unclothed, into the assembly' (65:35-36). The enemy chief begins to pull at Draupadi's sari. Draupadi silently prays to the incarnate Krishna. The Idea of Sustaining Law (Dharma) materializes itself as clothing, and as the king pulls and pulls at her sari, there seems to be more and more of it. Draupadi is infinitely clothed and cannot be publicly stripped. It is one of Krishna's miracles.

Mahasweta's story rewrites this episode. The men easily succeed in stripping Dopdi—in the narrative it is the culmination of her political punishment by the representatives of the law. She remains publicly naked at her own insistence. Rather than save her modesty through the implicit intervention of a benign and divine (in this case it would have been godlike) comrade, the story insists that this is the place where male leadership stops.

It would be a mistake, I think, to read the modern story as a refutation of the ancient. Dopdi is (as heroic as) Draupadi. She is also what Draupadi—written into the patriarchal and authoritative sacred text as proof of male power—could not be. Dopdi is at once a palimpsest and a contradiction.

There is nothing 'historically implausible' about Dopdi's attitudes. When we first see her, she is thinking about washing her hair. She loves her husband and keeps political faith as an act of faith toward him. She adores her fore*fathers* because they protected their women's honour. (It should be recalled that this is thought in the context of American soldiers breeding bastards.) It is when she crosses the sexual differential into the field of what could *only happen to a woman* that she emerges as the most powerful 'subject,' who, still using the language of sexual 'honour,' can derisively call herself 'the object of your search,' whom the author can describe as a terrifying superobject—'an unarmed target'.

As a tribal, Dopdi is not romanticized by Mahasweta.

The decision makers among the revolutionaries are, again, 'realistically,' bourgeois young men and women who have oriented their book learning to the land and thus begun the long process of undoing the opposition between book (theory or 'outside') and spontaneity (practice or 'inside'). Such fighters are the hardest to beat, for they are neither tribal nor gentlemen. A Bengali reader would pick them out by name among the characters: the one with the aliases who bit off his tongue, the ones who helped the couple escape the army cordon; the ones who neither smoke nor drink tea; and, above all, Arijit. His is a fashionable name, tinsel Sanskrit, with no allusive paleonymy and a meaning that fits the story a bit too well: victorious over enemies. Yet it *is* his voice that gives Dopdi the courage to save not herself but her comrades.

Of course, this voice of male authority also fades. Once Dopdi enters, in the final section of the story, the postscript area of lunar flux and sexual difference, she is in a place where she will finally act *for* herself in *not* 'acting,' in challenging the man to (en)counter her as unrecorded or misrecorded objective historical monument. The army officer is shown as unable to ask the authoritative ontological question, What is this? In fact, in the sentence describing Dopdi's final summons to the sahib's tent, the agent is missing. I can be forgiven if I find in this an allegory of the woman's struggle within the revolution in a shifting historical moment.

As Mahasweta points out in an aside, the tribe in question is the Santal, not to be confused with at least nine other Munda tribes that inhabit India. They are also not to be confused with the so-called untouchables, who, unlike the tribals, are Hindu, though probably of remote 'non-Aryan' origin. In giving the name *Harijan* ('God's people') to the untouchables, Mahatma Gandhi had tried to concoct the sort of pride and sense of unity that the tribes seem to possess. Mahasweta has followed the Bengali practice of calling each so-called untouchable caste by the name of its menial and unclean task within the rigid structural functionalism of institutionalized Hinduism.[18] I have been unable to reproduce this in my translation.

Mahasweta uses another differentiation, almost on the level of caricature: the Sikh and the Bengali. (Sikhism was founded as a reformed religion by Guru Nanak in the late fifteenth century. Today the roughly nine million Sikhs of India live chiefly in East Punjab, at the other end of the vast Indo-Gangetic Plain from Bengal. The tall, muscular, turbanned, and bearded Sikh, so unlike the slight and supposedly intellectual Bengali, is the stereotyped butt of jokes in the same way as the Polish community in North America or the Belgian in France.) Arjan Singh, the diabetic Sikh captain who falls back on the *Granth-sahib* (the Sikh sacred book—I have translated it 'Scripture') and the 'five Ks' of the Sikh religion, is presented as all brawn and no brains; and the wily, imaginative, corrupt Bengali Senanayak is, of course, the army officer full of a Keatsian negative capability.[19]

The entire energy of the story seems, in one reading, directed toward breaking the apparently clean gap between theory and practice in Senanayak. Such a clean break is not possible, of course. The theoretical production of negative capability is a practice; the practice of mowing down Naxalites brings with it a theory of the historical moment. The assumption of such a clean break in fact depends upon the assumption that the individual subject who theorizes and practices is in full control. At least in the history of the Indo-European tradition in general, such a sovereign subject is also the legal or legitimate subject, who is identical with his stable patronymic.[20] It might therefore be interesting that Senanayak is not given the differentiation of a first name and surname. His patronymic is identical with his function (not of course by the law of caste): the common noun means 'army chief.' In fact, there is the least hint of a doubt if it is a proper name or a common appellation. This may be a critique of the man's apparently self-adequate identity, which sustains his theory-practice juggling act. If so, it goes with what I see as the project of the story: to break this bonded identity with the wedge of an *unreasonable* fear. If our certitude of the efficient-information-retrieval and talk-to-the-accessible approach toward Third-World women can be broken by the wedge of an unreasonable uncertainty, into a feeling that what we deem gain might spell loss and that our practice should be forged accordingly, then we would share the textual effect of 'Draupadi' with Senanayak.

The italicized words in the translation are in English in the original. It is to be noticed that the fighting words on both sides are in English. Nation-state politics combined with multinational economies produce war. The language of war—offence *and* defence—is international. English is standing in here for that nameless and heterogeneous world language. The peculiarities of usage belong to being obliged to cope with English under political and social pressure for a few centuries. Where, indeed, is there a 'pure' language? given the nature of the struggle, there is nothing bizarre in 'Comrade Dopdi.'[21] It is part of the undoing of opposites—intellectual-rural, tribalist-internationalist—that is the wavering constitution of 'the underground,' 'the wrong side' of the law. On the right side of the law, such deconstructions, breaking down national distinctions, are operated through the encroachment of king-emperor or capital.

The only exception is the word 'sahib.' An Urdu word meaning 'friend,' it came to mean, almost exclusively in Bengali, 'white man.' It is a colonial word and is used today to mean 'boss.' I thought of Kipling as I wrote 'Burra Sahib' for Senanayak.

In the matter of 'translation' between Bengali and English it is again Dopdi who occupies a curious middle space. She is the only one who uses the word 'kounter' (the 'n' is no more than a nasalization of the diphthong 'ou'). As Mahasweta explains, it is an abbreviation for 'killed by police in an encounter,' the code description for death by police torture. Dopdi does not understand English, but she understands this formula and the word. In her use of it at the end, it comes mysteriously close to the 'proper' English usage. It is the menacing appeal of the objectified subject to its politico-sexual enemy—the provisionally silenced master of the subject-object dialectic—to encounter—'kounter'—her. What is it to 'use' a language 'correctly' without 'knowing' it?

We cannot answer because we, with Senanayak, are in the opposite situation. Although we are told of specialists, the meaning of Dopdi's song remains undisclosed in the text. The educated Bengali does not know the languages of the tribes, and no political coercion obliges him to 'know' it. What one might falsely think of as a political 'privilege'—knowing English properly—stands in the way of a deconstructive practice of language—using it 'correctly' through a political displacement, or operating the language of the other side.

It follows that I have had the usual 'translator's problems' only with the peculiar Bengali spoken by the tribals. In general we educated Bengalis have the same racist attitude toward it as the late Peter Sellers had toward our English. It would have been embarrassing to have used some version of the language of D. H. Lawrence's 'common people' or Faulkner's Blacks. Again, the specificity is micrological. I have used 'straight English,' whatever that may be.

Notes

1. Reproduced from Spivak, *In Other Worlds: Essays in Cultural Politics* (New York and London: Methuen, 1987). Updated and lightly edited.

2. For elaborations upon such a suggestion, see Jean-Francois Lyotard, *The Postmodern Condition: A Report on Knowledge* (Minneapolis: Minnesota University Press, 1984).

3. See my 'Three Feminist Readings: McCullers, Drabble, Habermas,' *Union Seminary Quarterly Review* 1–2 (Fall–Winter 1979–80), and 'French Feminism in an International Frame', Spivak, *In Other Worlds*, pp.134–53.

4. This list represents a distillation of suggestions to be found in the work of Jacques Derrida: see, e.g., 'The Exorbitant. Question of Method,' *Of Grammatology*, tr. Spivak; 'Limited Inc,' tr. Samuel Weber, *Glyph 2* (1977); 'Ou commence et comment finit un corps enseignant,' in *Politiques de la philosophie*, ed. Dominique Grisoni (Paris:B. Grasset, 1976);

and my 'Revolutions That as Yet Have No Model: Derrida's "Limited Inc,"' *Diacritics* 10 (Dec. 1980), and 'Sex and History in Wordsworth's *The Prelude* (1805) IX–XIII', Spivak, *In Other Worlds*, pp. 46–76.

5. It is a sign of E. M. Forster's acute perception of India that *A Passage to India* contains a glimpse of such an ex-orbitant tribal in the figure of the punkha puller in the courtroom.

6. Mahasweta Devi, *Agnigarbha* (Calcutta, 1978), p. 8.

7. For a discussion of the relationship between academic degrees in English and the production of revolutionary literature, see my 'A Vulgar Inquiry into the Relationship between Academic Criticism and Literary Production in West Bengal' (paper delivered at the Annual Convention of the Modern Language Association, Houston, 1980).

8. These figures are an average of the 1971 census in West Bengal and the projected figure for the 1974 census in Bangladesh.

9. See Dinesh Chandra Sen, *History of Bengali Language and Literature* (Calcutta, 1911). A sense of Bengali literary nationalism can be gained from the (doubtless apocryphal) report that, upon returning from his first investigative tour of India, Macaulay remarked: 'The British Crown presides over two great literatures: the English and the Bengali.'

10. See Gautam Chattopadhyay, *Communism and the Freedom Movement in Bengal* (New Delhi, 1970).

11. Marcus F. Franda, *Radical Politics in West Bengal* (Cambridge: MIT Press, 1971), p. 153. I am grateful to Michael Ryan for having located this accessible account of the Naxalbari movement. There now exists an excellent study by Sumanta Banerjee, *India's Simmering Revolution: The Naxalite Uprising* (London: Zed Press, 1984).

12. See Samar Sen, et al., eds., *Naxalbari and After: a Frontier Anthology*, 2 vols. (Calcutta, 1978).

13. See Bernard-Henri Lévy, *Bangla Desh: Nationalisme dans la révolution* (Paris, 1973).

14. Franda, *Radical Politics*, pp. 163–64. see also p. 164, n.22.

15. Lawrence Lifschultz, *Bangladesh: The Unfinished Revolution* (London: Zed Press, 1979), pp. 25, 26.

16. For my understanding of this aspect of the *Mahabharata,* I am indebted to Romila Thapar of Jawaharlal Nehru University, New Delhi.

17. I borrow this sense of singularity from Jacques Lacan, 'Seminar on "The Purloined Letter",' tr. Jeffrey Mehlman, *Yale French Studies* 48 (1972): 53, 59.

18. As a result of the imposition of the capitalist mode of production and the Imperial Civil Service, and massive conversions of the lowest castes to Christianity, the invariable identity of caste and trade no longer holds. Here, too, there is the possibility of a taxonomy micrologically deconstructive of the caste-class oposition, functioning heterogeneously in terms of the social hierarchy.

19. If indeed the model for this character is Ranjit Gupta, the notorious Inspector General of police of West Bengal, the delicate textuality, in the interest of a political position, of Senanayak's delineation in the story takes us far beyond the limits of a reference *a clef.* I am grateful to Michael Ryan for suggesting the possibility of such a reference.

20. The relationship between phallocentrism, the patriarchy, and clean binary oppositions is a pervasive theme in Derrida's critique of the metaphysics of presence. see my 'Unmaking and Making in *To the Lighthouse*', Spivak, *In Other Worlds*, pp. 30–45.

21. 'My dearest Sati, through the walls and the miles that separate us I can hear you saying, "In Sawan it will be two years since Comrade left us." The other women will nod. It is you who have taught them the meaning of Comrade' (Mary Tyler, 'Letter to a Former Cell-Mate,' in *Naxalbari and After,* 1:307; see also Tyler, *My Years in an Indian Prison* [Harmondsworth: Penguin, 1977]).

draupadi

mahasweta devi

NAME DOPDI MEJHEN, age twenty-seven, husband Dulna Majhi (deceased), domicile Cherakhan, Bankrahjarh, infor-mation whether dead or alive and/or assistance in arrest, one hundred rupees . . .

An exchange between two medallioned *uniforms.*

FIRST MEDALLION: What's this, a tribal called Dopdi? The list of names I brought has nothing like it! How can anyone have an unlisted name?

SECOND: Draupadi Mejhen. Born the year her mother threshed rice at Surja Sahu (killed)'s at Bakuli. Surja Sahu's wife gave her the name.

FIRST: These officers like nothing better than to write as much as they can in English. What's all this stuff about her?

SECOND: *Most notorious* female. *Long wanted in many . . .*

Dossier: Dulna and Dopdi worked at harvests, *rotating* between Birbhum, Burdwan, Murshidabad, and Bankura. In 1971, in the famous *Operation* Bakuli, when three villages were *cordonned* off and *machine gunned,* they too lay on the ground, faking dead. In fact, they were the main culprits. Murdering Surja Sahu and his son, occupying upper-caste wells and tubewells during the drought, not surrendering those three young men to the police. In all this they were the chief instigators. In the morning, at the time of the body count, the couple could not be found. The blood-sugar level of Captain Arjan Singh, the *architect* of Bakuli, rose at once and proved yet again that diabetes can be a result of anxiety and depression. Diabetes has twelve husbands—among them anxiety.

Dulna and Dopdi went underground for a long time in a *Neanderthal* darkness. The Special Forces, attempting to pierce that dark by an armed search, compelled quite a few Santals in the various districts of West Bengal to meet their Maker against their will. By the Indian Constitution, all human beings, regardless of caste or creed, are sacred. Still, accidents like this do happen. Two sorts of reasons: (1) the underground couple's skill in self-concealment; (2) not merely the Santals but all tribals of the Austro-Asiatic Munda tribes appear the same to the Special Forces.

In fact, all around the ill-famed forest of Jharkhani, which is under the jurisdiction of the police station at Bankrajharh (in this India of ours, even a worm is under a certain police station), even in the southeast and southwest corners, one comes across hair-raising details in the eyewitness records put together on the people who are suspected of attacking police stations, stealing guns (since the snatchers are not invariably well educated, they sometimes say 'give up your *chambers*' rather than give up your gun), killing grain brokers, landlords, moneylenders, law officers, and bureaucrats. A black-skinned couple ululated like police *sirens* before the episode. They sang jubiliantly in a savage tongue, incomprehensible even to the Santals. Such as:

Samaray hijulenako mar goekope

and,

Hendre rambra keche keche
Pundi rambra keche keche

This proves conclusively that they are the cause of Captain Arjan Singh's diabetes.

Government procedure being as incomprehensible as the Male Principle in Sankhya philosophy or Antonioni's early films, it was Arjan Singh who was sent once again on *Operation Forest* Jharkhani. Learning from Intelligence that the above-mentioned ululating and dancing couple was the escaped corpses, Arjan Singh fell for a bit into a *zombie* like state and finally acquired so irrational a dread of black-skinned people that whenever he saw a black person in a ball-bag, he swooned, saying 'they're killing me,' and drank and passed a lot of water. Neither uniform nor Scriptures could relieve that depression. At long last, under the shadow of a *premature and forced retirement,* it was possible to present him at the desk of Mr Senanayak, the elderly Bengali specialist in combat and extreme-Left politics.

Senanayak knows the activities and capacities of the

opposition better than they themselves do. First, therefore, he presents an encomium on the military genius of the Sikhs. Then he explains further: is it only the opposition that should find power at the end of the barrel of a gun? Arjan Singh's power also explodes out of the *male organ* of a gun. Without a gun even the 'five Ks'[1] come to nothing in this day and age. These speeches he delivers to all and sundry. As a result, the fighting forces regain their confidence in the *Army Handbook.* It is not a book for everyone. It says that the most despicable and repulsive style of fighting is guerrilla warfare with primitive weapons. Annihilation at sight of any and all practitioners of such warfare is the sacred duty of every soldier. Dopdi and Dulna belong to the *category* of such fighters, for they too kill by means of hatchet and scythe, bow and arrow, etc. In fact, their fighting power is greater than the gentlemen's. Not all gentlemen become experts in the explosion of 'chambers'; they think the power will come out on its own if the gun is held. But since Dulna and Dopdi are illiterate, their kind have practised the use of weapons generation after generation.

I should mention here that, although the other side make little of him, Senanayak is not to be trifled with. Whatever his *practice,* in *theory* he respects the opposition. Respects them because they could be neither understood nor demolished if they were treated with the attitude, 'it's nothing but a bit of impertinent game-playing with guns.' *In order to destroy the enemy, become one.* Thus he understood them by (*theoretically*) becoming one of them. He hopes to write on all this in the future. He has also decided that in his written work he will demolish the gentlemen and *highlight* the message of the harvest workers. These mental processes might seem complicated, but actually he is a simple man and is as pleased as his third great-uncle after a meal of turtle meat. In fact, he knows that, as in the old popular song, turn by turn the world will change. And in every world he must have the credentials to survive with honour. If necessary he will show the future to what extent he alone understands the matter in its proper perspective. He knows very well that what he is doing today the future will forget, but he also knows that if he can change colour from world to world, he can represent the particular world in question. Today he is getting rid of the young by means of *'apprehension and elimination,'* but he knows people will soon forget the memory and lesson of blood. And at the same time, he, like Shakespeare, believes in delivering the world's *legacy* into youth's hands. He is Prospero as well.

At any rate, information is received that many young men and women, *batch by batch* and on jeeps, have attacked police station after police station, terrified and elated the region, and disappeared into the forest of Jharkhani. Since after escaping from Bakuli, Dopdi and Dulna have worked at the house of virtually every landowner, they can efficiently inform the killers about their targets and announce proudly that they too are soldiers, *rank and file.* Finally the impenetrable forest of Jharkhani is surrounded by real soldiers, the *army* enters and splits the battlefield. Soldiers in hiding guard the falls and springs that are the only source of drinking water; they are still guarding, still looking. On one such search, army informant Dukhiram Gharari saw a young Santal man lying on his stomach on a flat stone, dipping his face to drink water. The soldiers shot him as he lay.

As the .303 threw him off spread-eagled and brought a bloody foam to his mouth, he roared 'Ma—ho' and then went limp. They realized later that it was the redoubtable Dulna Majhi.

What does 'Ma-ho' mean? Is this a violent slogan in the tribal language? Even after much thought, the Department of Defence could not be sure. Two tribal-specialist types are flown in from Calcutta, and they sweat over the dictionaries put together by worthies such as Hoffman-Jeffer and Golden-Palmer. Finally the omniscient Senanayak summons Chamru, the water carrier of the *camp*. He giggles when he sees the two specialists, scratches his ear with his 'bidi', and says, the Santals of Maldah did say that when they began fighting at the time of King Gandhi! It's a battle cry. Who said 'Ma—ho' here? Did someone come from Maldah?

The problem is thus solved. Then, leaving Dulna's body on the stone, the soldiers climb the trees in green camouflage. They embrace the leafy boughs like so many great god Pans and wait as the large red ants bite their private parts. To see if anyone comes to take away the body. This is the hunter's way, not the soldier's. But Senanayak knows that these brutes cannot be dispatched by the approved method. So he asks his men to draw the prey with a corpse as bait. All will come clear, he says. I have almost deciphered Dopdi's song.

The soldiers get going at his command. But no one comes to claim Dulna's corpse. At night the soldiers shoot at a scuffle and, descending, discover that they have killed two hedgehogs copulating on dry leaves. Improvidently enough, the soldiers' jungle scout Dukhiram gets a knife in the neck before he can claim the reward for Dulna's capture. Bearing Dulna's corpse, the soldiers suffer shooting pains as the ants, interrupted in their feast, begin to bite them. When Senanayak hears that no one has come to take the corpse, he slaps his *anti-Fascist paperback* copy of *The Deputy* and snouts, '*What*?' Immediately one of the tribal specialists runs in with a joy as naked and transparent as Archimedes' and says, 'Get up, *sir*! I have discovered the meaning of that 'hende rambra' stuff. It's Mundari *language*.

Thus the search for Dopdi continues. In the forest *belt* of Jharkhani, the *Operation* continues—will continue. It is a carbuncle on the government's backside. Not to be cured by the tested ointment, not to burst with the appropriate herb. In the first phase the fugitives, ignorant of the forest's topography, are caught easily, and by the law of confrontation they are shot at the taxpayer's expense. By the law of confrontation, their eyeballs, intestines, stomachs, hearts, genitals, and so on become the food of fox, vulture, hyena, wildcat, ant, and worm, and the untouchables go off happily to sell their bare skeletons.

They do not allow themselves to be captured in open combat in the next phase. Now it seems that they have found a trustworthy courier. Ten to one it's Dopdi. Dopdi loved Dulna more than her blood. No doubt it is she who is saving the fugitives now.

'They' is also a *hypothesis*.

Why?

How many went *originally*?

The answer is silence. About that there are many tales, many books in press. Best not to believe everything.

How many killed in six years' confrontation?

The answer is silence.

Why after confrontations are the skeletons discovered with arms broken or severed? Could armless men have fought? Why do the collarbones shake, why are legs and ribs crushed?

Two kinds of answer. Silence. Hurt rebuke in the eyes. Shame on you! Why bring this up? What will be will be . . .

How many left in the forest? The answer is silence.

A *legion*? Is it *justifiable* to maintain a large battalion in that wild area at the taxpayers' expense?

Answer: *Objection.* 'Wild area' is incorrect. The battalion is provided with supervised nutrition, arrangements to worship according to religion, opportunity to listen to 'Bibidha Bharati'[2] and to see Sanjeev Kumar and the Lord Krishna face-to-face in the movie *This is Life.*[2] No. The area is not wild.

How many are left?

The answer is silence.

How many are left? Is there anyone *at all*?

The answer is long.

Item: *Well, action* still goes on. Moneylenders, landlords, grain brokers, anonymous brothel keepers, ex-informants are still terrified. The hungry and naked are still defiant and irrepressible. In some *pockets* the harvest workers are getting a *better wage.* Villages sympathetic to the fugitives are still silent and hostile. These events cause one to think . . .

Where in this picture does Dopdi Mejhen fit?

She must have connections with the fugitives. The cause for fear is elsewhere. The ones who remain have lived a long time in the primitive world of the forest. They keep company with the poor harvest workers and the tribals. They must have forgotten book learning. Perhaps they are *orienting* their book learning to the soil they live on and learning new combat and survival techniques. One can shoot and get rid of the ones whose only recourse is extrinsic book learning and sincere intrinsic enthusiasm. Those who are working practically will not be exterminated so easily.

Therefore *Operation* Jharkhani *Forest* cannot stop. Reason: the words of warning in the *Army Handbook.*

2

Catch Dopdi Mejhen. She will lead us to the others.

Dopdi was proceeding slowly, with some rice knotted into her belt. Mushai Tudu's wife had cooked her some. She does so occasionally. When the rice is cold, Dopdi knots it into her waistcloth and walks slowly. As she walked, she picked out and killed the lice in her hair. If she had some *kerosene,* she'd rub it into her scalp and get rid of her lice. Then she could wash her hair with baking soda. But the bastards put traps at every bend of the falls. If they smell *kerosene* in the water, they will follow the scent.

Dopdi!

She doesn't respond. She never responds when she hears her own name. She has seen in the Panchayat[3] office just today the notice for the reward in her name. Mushai Tudu's wife had said, 'What are you looking at? Who is Dopdi Mejhen! Money if you give her up!'

'How much?'

'Two—hundred!'

Oh God!

Mushai's wife said outside the office: 'A lot of

preparation this time. A—ll new policemen."

Hm.

Don't come again.

Why?

Mushai's wife looked down. Tudu says that Sahib has come again. If they catch you, the village, our huts . . .

They'll burn again.

Yes. And about Dukhiram.

The Sahib knows?

Shomai and Budhna betrayed us.

Where are they?

Ran away by train.

Dopdi thought of something. Then said, Go home. I don't know what will happen, if they catch me don't know me.

Can't you run away?

No. Tell me, how many times can I run away? What will they do if they catch me? They will *kounter* me. Let them.

Mushai's wife said, We have nowhere else to go.

Dopdi said softly, I won't tell anyone's name.

Dopdi knows, has learned by hearing so often and so long, how one can come to terms with torture. If mind and body give way under torture, Dopdi will bite off her tongue. That boy did it. They kountered him. When they kounter you, your hands are tied behind you. All your bones are crushed, your sex is a terrible wound. *Killed by police in an encounter . . . unknown male . . . age twenty-two . . .*

As she walked thinking these thoughts, Dopdi heard someone calling, Dopdi!

She didn't respond. She doesn't respond if called by her own name. Here her name is Upi Mejhen. But who calls?

Spines of suspicion are always furled in her mind. Hearing 'Dopdi' they stiffen like a hedgehog's. Walking, she *unrolls the film* of known faces in her mind. Who? No Shomra, Shomra is on the run. Shomai and Budhna are also on the run, for other reasons. Not Golok, he is in Bakuli. Is it someone from Bakuli? After Bakuli, her and Dulna's names were Upi Mejhen, Matang Majhi. Here no one but Mushai and his wife knows their real names. Among the young gentlemen, not all of the previous *batches* knew.

That was a troubled time. Dopdi is confused when she thinks about it. *Operation* Bakuli in Bakuli. Surja Sahu arranged with Biddibabu to dig two tubewells and three wells within the compound of his two houses. No water anywhere, drought in Birbhum. Unlimited water at Surja Sahu's house, as clear as a crow's eye.

Get your water with canal tax, everything is burning.

What's my profit in increasing cultivation with tax money?

Everything's on fire.

Get out of here. I don't accept your Panchayat nonsense. Increase cultivation with water. You want half the paddy for sharecropping. Everyone is happy with free paddy. Then give me paddy at home, give me money, I've learned my lesson trying to do you good.

What good did you do?

Have I not given water to the village?

You've given it to your kin Bhagunal.

Don't you get water?

No. The untouchables don't get water.

The quarrel began there. In the drought, human patience catches easily. Satish and Jugal from the village and that young gentleman, was Rana his name? said a landowning moneylender won't give a thing, put him down.

Surja Sahu's house was surrounded at night. Surja Sahu had brought out his gun. Surja was tied up with cow rope. His whitish eyeballs turned and turned, he was incontinent again and again. Dulna had said, I'll have the first blow, brothers. My great-grandfather took a bit of paddy from him, and I still give him free labour to repay that debt.

Dopdi had said, His mouth watered when he looked at me. I'll put out his eyes.

Surja Sahu. Then a *telegraphic message* from Shiuri. *Special train. Army.* The *jeep* didn't come up to Bakuli. *March-march-march.* The *crunch-crunch-crunch* of gravel under hobnailed boots. *Cordon up: Commands* on the *mike.* Jugal Mandal, Satish Mandal, Rana *alias* Prabir *alias* Dipak, Dulna Majhi-Dopdi Mejhen *surrender surrender surrender. No surrender surrender. Mow-mow-mow down the village.* Putt-putt-putt-putt—*cordite* in the air—putt-putt—*round the clock*—putt-putt. *Flame thrower.* Bakuli is burning. *More men and women, children . . . fire—fire. Close canal approach. Over-over-over by nightfall.* Dopdi and Dulna had crawled on their stomachs to safety.

They could not have reached Paltakuri after Bakuli. Bhupati and Tapa took them. Then it was decided that Dopdi and Dulna would work around the Jharkhani *belt.* Dulna had explained to Dopdi, Dear this is best! We won't get family and children this way. But who knows? Landowner and moneylender and policemen might one day be wiped out!

Who called her from the back today?

Dopdi kept walking. Villages and fields, bush and

rock—*Public Works Department* markers—sound of running steps in back. Only one person running. Jharkhani Forest still about two miles away. Now she thinks of nothing but entering the forest. She must let them know that the *police* have set up *notices* for her again. Must tell them that that bastard Sahib has appeared again. Must change *hideouts.* Also, the *plan* to do to Lakkhi Bera and Naran Bera what they did to Surja Sahu on account of the trouble over paying the field hands in Sandara must be cancelled. Shomai and Budhna knew everything. There was the *urgency* of great danger under Dopdi's ribs. Now she thought there was no shame as a Santal in Shomai and Budhna's treachery. Dopdi's blood was the pure unadulterated black blood of Champabhumi.[4] From Champa to Bakuli the rise and set of a million moons. The blood could have been contaminated; Dopdi felt proud of her forefathers. They stood guard over their women's blood in black armour. Shomai and Budhna are half-breeds. The fruits of war. Contributions to Radhabhumi by the American soldiers stationed at Shiandange. Otherwise crow would eat crow's flesh before Santal would betray Santal.

Footsteps at her back. The steps keep a distance. Rice in her belt, tobacco leaves tucked at her waist. Arijit, Malini, Shamu, Mantu—none of them smokes or even drinks tea. Tobacco leaves and limestone powder. Best medicine for scorpion bite. Nothing must be given away.

Dopdi turned left. This way is the *camp.* Two miles. This is not the way to the forest. But Dopdi will not enter the forest with a cop at her back.

I swear by my life. By my life Dulna, by my life. Nothing must be told.

The footsteps turn left. Dopdi touches her waist. In her palm the comfort of a half-moon. A baby scythe. The smiths at Jharkhani are fine artisans. Such an edge we'll put on it Upi, a hundred Dukhirams—Thank God Dopdi is not a gentleman. Actually, perhaps they have understood scythe, hatchet, and knife best. They do their work in silence. The lights of the *camp* at a distance. Why is Dopdi going this way? Stop a bit, it turns again. Huh! I can tell where I am if I wander all night with my eyes shut. I won't go in the forest, I won't lose him that way. I won't outrun him. You fucking jackal[5] of a cop, deadly afraid of death, you can't run around in the forest. I'd run you out of breath, throw you in a ditch, and finish you off.

Not a word must be said. Dopdi has seen the new *camp,* she has sat in the *bus station,* passed the time of day, smoked a 'bidi' and found out how many *police convoys* had arrived, how many *radio vans.* Squash four, onions seven, peppers fifty, a straightforward account. This information cannot now be passed on. They will understand Dopdi Mejhen has been kountered. Then they'll run. Arijit's voice. If anyone is caught, the others must catch the *timing* and *change* their *hideout.* If *Comrade* Dopdi arrives late, we will not remain. There will be a sign of where we've gone. No *comrade*[6] will let the others be destroyed for her own sake.

Arijit's voice. The gurgle of water. The direction of the next *hideout* will be indicated by the tip of the wooden arrowhead under the stone.

Dopdi likes and understands this. Dulna died, but, let me tell you, he didn't lose anyone else's life. Because this was not in our heads to begin with, one was kountered for the other's trouble. Now a much harsher rule, easy and clear. Dopdi returns—good; doesn't return—*bad. Change hideout.* The clue will be such that the opposition won't see it, won't understand even if they do.

Footsteps at her back. Dopdi turns again. These three and a half miles of land and rocky ground are the best way to enter the forest. Dopdi has left that way behind. A little level ground ahead. Then rocks again. The *army* could not have struck *camp* on such rocky terrain. This area is quiet enough. It's like a maze, every hump looks like every other. That's fine. Dopdi will lead the cop to the burning 'ghat'. Patitpaban of Saranda had been sacrificed in the name of Kali of the Burning Ghats.

Apprehend!

A lump of rock stands up. Another. Yet another. The elder Senanayak was at once triumphant and despondent. *If you want to destroy the enemy, become one.* He had done so. As long as six years ago he could anticipate their every move. He still can. Therefore he is elated. Since he has kept up with the literature, he has read *First Blood* and seen approval of his thought and work.

Dopdi couldn't trick him, he is unhappy about that. Two sorts of reasons. Six years ago he published an article about information storage in brain cells. He demonstrated in that piece that he supported this struggle from the point of view of the field hands. Dopdi is a field hand. *Veteran fighter. Search and destroy* Dopdi Mejhen is about to be *apprehended.* Will be *destroyed.* Regret.

Halt!

Dopdi stops short. The steps behind come around to the front. Under Dopdi's ribs the *canal* dam breaks.

No hope. Surja Sahu's brother Rotoni Sahu. The two lumps of rock come forward. Shomai and Budhna. They had not escaped by train.

Arijit's voice. Just as you must know when you've won, you must also acknowledge defeat and start the activities of the next *stage*.

Now Dopdi spreads her arms, raises her face to the sky, turns toward the forest, and ululates with the force of her entire being. Once, twice, three times. At the third burst the birds in the trees at the outskirts of the forest awake and flap their wings. The echo of the call travels far.

3

Draupadi Mejhen was apprehended at 6:53 p.m. It took an hour to get her to *camp*. Questioning took another hour exactly. No one touched her, and she was allowed to sit on a canvas camp stool. At 8:57 Senanayak's dinner hour approached, and saying, 'Make her. Do *the needful*,' he disappeared.

Then a billion moons pass. A billion lunar years. Opening her eyes after a million light years, Draupadi, strangely enough, sees sky and moon. Slowly the bloodied nailheads shift from her brain. Trying to move, she feels her arms and legs still tied to four posts. Something sticky under her ass and waist. Her own blood. Only the gag has been removed. Incredible thirst. In case she says 'water' she catches her lower lip in her teeth. She senses that her vagina is bleeding. How many came to make her?

Shaming her, a tear trickles out of the corner of her eye. In the muddy moonlight she lowers her lightless eye, sees her breasts, and understands that, indeed, she's made up right. Her breasts are bitten raw, the nipples torn. How many? Four-five-six-seven—then Draupadi had passed out.

She turns her eyes and sees something white. Her own cloth.[7] Nothing else. Suddenly she hopes against hope. Perhaps they have abandoned her. For the foxes to devour. But she hears the scrape of feet. She turns her head, the guard leans on his bayonet and leers at her. Draupadi closes her eyes. She doesn't have to wait long. Again the process of making her begins. Goes on. The moon vomits a bit of light and goes to sleep. Only the dark remains. A compelled spread-eagled still body. Active *pistons* of flesh rise and fall, rise and fall over it.

Then morning comes.

Then Draupadi Mejhen is brought to the tent and thrown on the straw. Her piece of cloth is thrown over her body.

Then, after *breakfast*, after reading the newspaper and sending the radio message 'Draupadi Mejhen apprehended,' etc., Draupadi Mejhen is ordered brought in.

Suddenly there is trouble.

Draupadi sits up as soon as she hears 'Move!' and asks, Where do you want me to go?

To the Burra Sahib's tent.

Where is the tent?

Over there.

Draupadi fixes her red eyes on the tent. Says, Come, I'll go.

The guard pushes the water pot forward.

Draupadi stands up. She pours the water down on the ground. Tears her piece of cloth with her teeth.

Seeing such strange behaviour, the guard says, She's gone crazy, and runs for orders. He can lead the prisoner out but doesn't know what to do if the prisoner behaves incomprehensibly. So he goes to ask his superior.

The commotion is as if the alarm had sounded in a prison. Senanayak walks out surprised and sees Draupadi, naked, walking toward him in the bright sunlight with her head high. The nervous guards trail behind.

What is this? He is about to cry, but stops.

Draupadi stands before him, naked. Thigh and pubic hair matted with dry blood. Two breasts, two wounds.

What is this? He is about to bark.

Draupadi comes closer. Stands with her hand on her hip, laughs and says, The object of your search, Dopdi Mejhen. You asked them to make me up, don't you want to see how they made me?

Where are her clothes?

Won't put them on, *sir*. Tearing them.

Draupadi's black body comes even closer. Draupadi shakes with an indomitable laughter that Senanayak simply cannot understand. Her ravaged lips bleed as she begins laughing. Draupadi wipes the blood on her palm and says in a voice that is as terrifying, sky splitting, and sharp as her ululation, What's the use of clothes? You can strip me, but how can you clothe me again? Are you a man?

She looks around and chooses the front of Senanayak's white bush shirt to spit a bloody gob at and says, There isn't a man here that I should be ashamed. I will not let you put my cloth on me. What more can you do? Come on, *kounter* me—come on, *kounter* me—?

Draupadi pushes Senanayak with her two mangled breasts, and for the first time Senanayak is afraid to stand before an unarmed *target,* terribly afraid.

1981

Notes

I am grateful to Soumya Chakravarti for his help in solving occasional problems of English synonyms and archival research.

1. The 'five Ks' are *Kes* ('unshorn hair'); *kachh* ("drawers down to the knee"); *karha*('iron bangle'); *kirpan* ('dagger'); *kanga* ('comb'); to be worn by every Sikh, hence a mark of identity.

2. 'Bibidha Bharati' is a popular radio program, on which listeners can hear music of their choice. The Hindi film industry is prolific in producing pulp movies for consumption in India and in all parts of the world where there is an Indian, Pakistani, and West Indian labour force. Many of the films are adaptations from the epics. Sanjeev Kumar is an idolized actor. Since it was Krishna who rescued Draupadi from her predicament in the epic, and, in the film the soldiers watch, Sanjeev Kumar encounters Krishna, there might be a touch of textual irony here.

3. 'Panchayat' is a supposedly elected body of village self-government.

4. 'Champabhumi' and 'Radhabhumi' are archaic names for certain areas of Bengal. 'Bhumi' is simply 'land' All of Bengal is thus 'Bangabhumi.'

5. The jackal following the tiger is a common image.

6. Modern Bengali does not distinguish between 'her' and 'his.' The 'her' in the sentence beginning 'No *comrade* will . . .' can therefore be considered an interpretation.

7. A *sari* conjures up the long many-pleated piece of cloth, complete with blouse and underclothes, that 'proper' Indian women wear. Dopdi wears a much-abbreviated version, without blouse or underclothes. It is referred to simply as 'the cloth.'

breast-giver

mahesweta devi

My aunties they lived in the woods,
in the forest their home they did make
Never did Aunt say here's a sweet dear,
eat sweetie, here's a piece of cake.

JASHODA DOESN'T REMEMBER if her aunt was kind or unkind. It is as if she were Kangalicharan's wife from birth, the mother of twenty children, living or dead, counted on her fingers. Jashoda doesn't remember at all when there was no child in her womb, when she didn't feel faint in morning, when Kangali's body didn't *drill* her body like a geologist in a darkness lit only by an oil-lamp. She never had the time to calculate if she could or could not bear motherhood. Motherhood was always her way of living and keeping alive her world of countless beings.

Jashoda was a mother by profession, *professional mother.* Jashoda was not an *amateur* mama like the daughters and wives of the master's house. The world belongs to the professional. In this city, this kingdom, the amateur beggar-pickpocket-hooker has no place. Even the mongrel on the path or side-walk, the greedy crow at the garbage don't make room for the upstart *amateur.* Jashoda had taken motherhood as her profession.

The responsibility was Mr Haldar's new son-in-law's Studebaker and the sudden desire of the youngest son of the Haldar-house to be a driver. When the boy suddenly got a whim in mind or body, he could not rest unless he had satisfied it instantly. These sudden whims reared up in the loneliness of the afternoon and kept him at slave labour like the khalifa of Bagdad. What he had done so far on that account did not oblige Jashoda to choose motherhood as a profession.

One afternoon the boy, driven by lust, attacked the cook and the cook, since her body was heavy with rice, stolen fishheads, and turnip greens, and her body languid with sloth, lay back, saying, 'Yah, do what you like.' Thus did the incubus of Bagdad get off the boy's shoulders and he wept repentant tears, mumbling, 'Auntie, don't tell'. The cook—saying, 'What's there to tell?'—went quickly to sleep. She never told anything. She was sufficiently proud that her body had attracted the boy. But the thief thinks of the loot. The boy got worried at the improper supply of fish and fries in his dish. He considered that he'd be fucked if the cook gave him away. Therefore on another afternoon, driven by the Bagdad djinn, he stole his mother's ring, slipped it into the cook's pillowcase, raised a hue and cry, and got the cook kicked out. Another afternoon he lifted the radio set from his father's room and sold it. It was difficult for his parents to find the connection between the hour of the afternoon and the boy's behaviour, since his father had created him in the deepest night by the astrological calendar and the tradition of the Haldars of Harisal. In fact you enter the sixteenth century as you enter the gates of this house. To this day you take your wife by the astrological almanac. But these matters are mere blind alleys. Motherhood did not become Jashoda's profession for these afternoon-whims.

One afternoon, leaving the owner of the shop, Kangalicharan was returning home with a handful of stolen samosas and sweets under his dhoti. Thus he returns daily. He and Jashoda eat rice. Their three offspring return before dark and eat stale samosa and sweets. Kangalicharan stirs the seething vat of milk in the sweet shop and cooks and feeds 'food cooked by a good Brahmin' to those pilgrims at the Lionseated goddess's temple who are proud that they are not themselves 'fake Brahmins by sleight of hand'. Daily he lifts a bit of flour and such and makes life easier. When he puts food in his belly in the afternoon he feels a filial inclination towards Jashoda, and he goes to sleep after handling her capacious bosom. Coming home in the afternoon, Kangalicharan was thinking of his imminent pleasure and tasting paradise at the thought of his wife's large round breasts. He was picturing himself as a farsighted son of man as he thought that marrying a fresh young thing, not working her overmuch, and feeding her well led to pleasure in the afternoon. At such a moment the Halder son, complete with Studebaker, swerving by Kangalicharan, ran over his feet and shins.

Instantly a crowd gathered. It was an accident in front of the house after all, 'otherwise I'd have drawn blood', screamed Nabin, the pilgrim-guide. He guides the pilgrims to the Mother goddess of Shakti-power, his temper is hot in the afternoon sun. Hearing him roar, all the Haldars who were at home came out.The Haldar chief started thrashing his son, roaring, 'You'll kill a Brahmin, you bastard, you unthinking bull?' The youngest son-in-law breathed relief as he saw that his Studebaker was not much damaged and, to prove that he was better human material than the money rich, *culture*-poor in-laws, he said in a voice as fine as the finest muslin, 'Shall we let the man die? Shouldn't we take him to the hospital?'—Kangali's boss was also in the crowd at the temple and, seeing the samosas and sweets flung on the roadway was about to say, 'Eh Brahmin!! Stealing food?' Now he held his tongue and said, 'Do that *sir*.' The youngest son-in-law and the Haldar chief took Kangalicharan quickly to the hospital. The master felt deeply grieved. During the Second War, when he helped the anti-Fascist struggle of the Allies by buying and selling scrap iron—then Kangali was a mere lad. Reverence for Brahmins crawled in Mr Haldar's veins. If he couldn't get Chatterjeebabu in the morning he would touch the feet of Kangali, young enough to be his son, and put a pinch of dust from his chapped feet on his own tongue. Kangali and Jashoda came to his house on feast days and Jashoda was sent a gift of cloth and vermillion when his daughters-in-law were pregnant. Now he said to Kangali—'Kangali! don't worry son. You won't suffer as long as I'm around.' Now it was that he thought that Kangali's feet, being turned to ground meat, he would not be able to taste their dust. He was most unhappy at the thought and he started weeping as he said, 'What has the son of a bitch done.' He said to the doctor at the hospital, 'Do what you can! Don't worry about cash.'

But the doctors could not bring the feet back. Kangali returned as a lame Brahmin. Haldarbabu had a pair of crutches made. The very day Kangali returned home on crutches, he learned that food had come to Jashoda from the Haldar house every day. Nabin was third in rank among the pilgrim-guides. He could only claim thirteen percent of the goddess's food and so had an inferiority complex. Inspired by seeing Rama-Krishna in the movies a couple of times, he called the goddess 'my crazy one' and by the book of the Kali-worshippers kept his consciousness immersed in local spirits. He said to Kangali, 'I put flowers on the crazy one's feet in your name. She said I have a share in Kangali's house, he will get out of the hospital by that fact.' Speaking of this to Jashoda, Kangali said, 'What? When I wasn't there, you were getting it off with Nabin?' Jashoda then grabbed Kangali's suspicious head between the two hemispheres of the globe and said, 'Two maid servants from the big house slept here every day to guard me. Would I look at Nabin? Am I not your faithful wife?'

In fact Kangali heard of his wife's flaming devotion at the big house as well. Jashoda had fasted at the mother's temple, had gone through a female ritual, and had travelled to the outskirts to pray at the feet of the local guru. Finally the Lionseated came to her in a dream as a midwife carrying a *bag* and said, 'Don't worry. Your man will return.' Kangali was most overwhelmed by this. Haldarbabu said, ' See, Kangali? The bastard unbelievers say, the mother gives a dream, why togged as a midwife? I say, she creates as mother, and preserves as midwife.'

Then Kangali said, 'Sir! How shall I work at the sweetshop any longer. I can't stir the vat with my kerutches.[1] You are god. You are feeding so many people in so many ways. I am not begging. Find me a job.'

Haldarbabu said, 'Yes Kangali! I've kept you a spot. I'll make you a shop in the corner of my porch. The Lionseated is across the way! Pilgrims come and go. Put up a shop of dry sweets. Now there's a wedding in the house. It's my bastard seventh son's wedding. As long as there's no shop, I'll send you food.'

Hearing this, Kangali's mind took wing like a rainbug in the rainy season. He came home and told Jashoda, 'Remember Kalidasa's poem? You eat because there isn't, wouldn't have got if there was? That's my lot, chuck. Master says he'll put up a shop after his son's wedding. Until then he'll send us food. Would this have happened if I had legs? All is Mother's will, dear!'

Everyone is properly amazed that in this fallen age the wishes and wills of the Lionseated, herself found by a dream-command a hundred and fifty years ago, are circulating around Kangalicharan Patitundo. Haldarbabu's change of heart is also Mother's will. He lives in independent India, the India that makes no distinctions among people, kingdoms, languages, varieties of Brahmins, varieties of Kayasthas and so on. But he made his cash in the British era, when *Divide and Rule* was the policy. Haldarbabu's mentality was constructed then. Therefore he doesn't trust anyone—not a Punjabi-Oriya-Bihari-Gujarati-Marathi-Muslim. At the sight of an unfortunate Bihari child or a starvation-ridden Oriya beggar his flab-protected heart, located under a forty-two inch Gopal brand vest, does not itch with the rash of kindness. He is a succesful son of Harisal. When he sees a West Bengali fly he says, 'Tchah! at home even the flies were fat—in the bloody West everything is pinched-skinny.' All the temple people are struck that such a man is filling with the milk of human kindness toward the West Bengali Kangalicharan. For some time this news is the general talk. Haldarbabu is such a patriot that, if his nephews or grandsons read the lives of the nation's leaders in their schoolbook, he says to his employees, 'Nonsense! why do they make 'em read the lives of characters from Dhaka, Mymensingh, Jashore? Harisal is made of the bone of the martyr god. One day it will emerge that the *Vedas* and the *Upanishads* were also written in Harisal.' Now his employees tell him, 'You have had a *change of heart,* so much kindness for a West Bengali, you'll see there is divine *purpose* behind this.' The Boss is delighted. He laughs loudly and says 'there is no East or West for a Brahmin. If there's a sacred thread around his neck you have to give him respect even when he's taking a shit.'

Thus all around blow the sweet winds of sympathy-compassion-kindness. For a few days, whenever Nabin tries to think of the Lionseated, the heavy-breasted, languid-hipped body of Jashoda floats in his mind's eye. A slow rise spreads in his body at the thought that perhaps she is appearing in his dream as Jashoda, just as she appeared in Jashoda's as a midwife. The fifty percent pilgrim-guide says to him, 'Male and female both get this disease. Bind the root of a white forget-me-not in your ear when you take a piss.'

Nabin doesn't agree. One day he tells Kangali, 'As

the Mother's son I won't make a racket with Shakti-power. But I've thought of a plan. There's no problem with making a Hare Krishna racket. I tell you, get a Gopal in your dream. My Aunt brought a stony Gopal from Puri. I give it to you. You announce that you got it in a dream. You'll see there'll be a to-do in no time, money will roll in. Start for money, later you'll get devoted to Gopal.'

Kangali says, 'Shame, brother! Should one joke with gods?'

'Ah get lost,' Nabin scolds. Later it appears that Kangali would have done well to listen to Nabin. For Haldarbabu suddenly dies of heart failure. Shakespeare's *welkin* breaks on Kangali and Jashoda's head.

2

Haldarbabu truly left Kangali in the lurch. Those wishes of the Lionseated that were manifesting themselves around Kangali *via-media* Haldarbabu disappeared into the blue like the burning promises given by a political party before the election and became magically invisible like the heroine of a fantasy. A European witch's *bodkin* pricks the colored balloon of Kangali and Jashoda's dreams and the pair falls in deep trouble. At home, Gopal, Nepal and Radharani whine interminably for food and abuse their mother. It is very natural for children to cry so for grub. Ever since Kangalicharan's loss of feet they'd eaten the fancy food of the Haldar household. Kangali also longs for food and is shouted at for trying to put his head in Jashoda's chest in the way of Gopal, the Divine Son. Jashoda is fully an Indian woman, whose unreasonble, unreasoning, and unintelligent devotion to her husband and love for her children, whose unnatural renunciation and forgiveness, have been kept alive in the popular consciousness by all Indian women from Sati-Savitri-Sita through Nirupa Roy and Chand Osmani.[2] The creeps of the world understand by seeing such women that the old Indian tradition is still flowing free—they understand that it was with such women in mind that the following aphorisms have been composed—'A female's life hangs on like a turtle's'—'her heart breaks but no word is uttered'—'the woman will burn, her ashes will fly/ Only then will we sing her/ praise on high.' Frankly, Jashoda never once wants to blame her husband for the present misfortune. Her mother-love wells up for Kangali as much as for the children. She wants to become the earth and feed her crippled husband and helpless childern with a fulsome harvest. Sages did not write of this motherly feeling of Jashoda's for her husband. They explained female and male as Nature and the Human Principle. But this they did in the days of yore—when they entered this *peninsula* from another land. Such is the power of the Indian soil that all women turn into mothers here and all men remain immersed in the spirit of holy childhood. Each man the Holy Child and each women the Divine Mother. Even those who deny this and wish to slap *current posters* to the effect of the '*eternal she*'—'Mona Lisa'—'La passionaria'—'Simone de Beauvoir,' et cetera, over the old ones and look at women that way are, after all, Indian cubs. It is notable that the educated Babus desire all this from women outside the home. When they cross the threshold they want the Divine Mother in the words and conduct of the revolutionary ladies. The *process* is most complicated. Because he understood this the heroines of Saratchandra always fed the hero an extra mouthful of rice. The apparent simplicity of Saratchandra's and other similar writers' writings is actually very complex and to be thought of in the evening, peacefully after a glass of wood-apple juice. There is too much influence of fun and games in the lives of the people who traffic in studies and intellectualism in West Bengal and therefore they should stress the wood-apple correspondingly. We have no idea of the loss we are sustaining because we do not stress the wood-apple-type-herbal remedies correspondingly.

However, it's incorrect to cultivate the habit of repeated incursions into *by-lanes* as we tell Jashoda's life story. The reader's patience, unlike the cracks in Calcutta streets, will not widen by the decade. The real thing is that Jashoda was in a cleft stick. Of course they ate their fill during the Master's funeral days, but after everything was over Jashoda clasped Radharani to her bosom and went over to the big house. Her aim was to speak to the Mistress and ask for the cook's job in the vegetarian kitchen.

The Mistress really grieved for the Master. But the lawyer let her know that the Master had left her the proprietorship of this house and the right to the rice warehouse. Girding herself with those assurances, she has once again taken the rudder of the family empire. She had really felt the loss of fish and fish-head.[3] Now she sees that the best butter, the best milk sweets from the best shops, heavy cream, and the best variety of bananas can also keep the body going somehow. The

Mistress lights up her easychair. A six-months' babe in her lap, her grandson. So far six sons have married. Since the almanac approves of the taking of a wife almost every month of the year, the birth rooms in a row on the ground floor of the Mistress's house are hardly ever empty. The *lady doctor* and Sarala the midwife never leave the house. The Mistress has six daughters. They too breed every year and a half. So there is a constant *epidemic* of blanket-quilt-feeding spoon-bottle-oilcloth-*Johnson's baby powder*-bathing basin.

The Mistress was out of her mind trying to feed the boy. As if relieved to see Jashoda she said, 'You come like a god! Give her some milk, dear, I beg you. His mother's sick—such a brat, he won't touch a bottle.' Jashoda immediately suckled the boy and pacified him. At the Mistress's special request Jashoda stayed in the house until nine p.m. and suckled the Mistress's grandson again and again. The cook filled a big bowl with rice and curry for her own household. Jashoda said as she suckled the boy, 'Mother! The Master said many things. He is gone, so I don't think of them. But Mother! Your Brahmin-son does not have his two feet. I don't think for myself. But thinking of my husband and sons I say, give me any kind of job. Perhaps you'll let me cook in your household?'

'Let me see dear! Let me think and see.' The Mistress is not as sold on Brahmins as the Master was. She doesn't accept fully that Kangali lost his feet because of her son's afternoon whims. It was written for Kangali as well, otherwise why was he walking down the road in the blazing sun grinning from ear to ear? She looks in charmed envy at Jashoda's *mammal projections* and says, 'The good lord sent you down as the legendary Cow of Fulfillment. Pull the teat and milk flows! The ones I've brought to my house, haven't a quarter of this milk in their nipples!'

Jashoda says, 'How true Mother! Gopal was weaned when he was three. This one hadn't come to my belly yet. Still it was like a flood of milk. Where does it come from, Mother? I have no good food, no pampering!'

This produced a lot of talk among the women at night and the menfolk got to hear it too at night. The second son, whose wife was sick and whose son drank Jashoda's milk, was particularly uxorious. The difference between him and his brothers was that the brothers created progeny as soon as the almanac gave a good day, with love or lack of love, with irritation or thinking of the accounts at the works. The second son impregnates his wife at the same *frequency*, but behind it lies deep love. The wife is often pregnant, that is an act of God. But the second son is also interested in that the wife remain beautiful at the same time. He thinks a lot about how to *combine* multiple pregnancies and beauty, but he cannot fathom it. But today, hearing from his wife about Jashoda's surplus milk, the second son said all of a sudden, 'Way found.'

'Way to what?'

'Uh, the way to save you pain.'

'How? I'll be out of pain when you burn me. Can a year-breeder's health mend?'

'It will, it will, I've got a divine engine in my hands! You'll breed yearly *and* keep your body.'

The couple discussed. The husband entered his Mother's room in the morning and spoke in heavy whispers. At first the Mistress hemmed and hawed, but then she thought to herself and realized that the proposal was worth a million rupees. Daughters-in-law *will* be mothers. When they are mothers, they will suckle their children. Since they will be mothers as long as it's possible—progressive suckling will ruin their shape. Then if the sons look outside, or harass the maid-servants, she won't have a voice to object. Going out because they can't get it at home—this is just. If Jashoda becomes the infants' suckling-mother, her daily meals, clothes on feast days, and some monthly pay will be enough. The Mistress is constantly occupied with women's rituals. There Jashoda can act as the fruitful Brahmin wife. Since Jashoda's misfortune is due to her son, that sin too will be lightened.

Jashoda received a portfolio when she heard her proposal. She thought of her breasts as most precious objects. At nights when Kangalicharan started to give her a feel she said, 'Look. I'm going to pull our weight with these. Take good care how you use them.' Kangalicharan hemmed and hawed that night, of course, but his Gopal frame of mind disappeared instantly when he saw the amounts of grains-oil-vegetables coming from the big house. He was illuminated by the spirit of Brahma the Creator and explained to Jashoda, 'You'll have milk in your breasts only if you have a child in your belly. Now you'll have to think of that and suffer. You are a faithful wife, a goddess. You will yourself be pregnant, be filled with a child, rear it at your breast, isn't this why Mother came to you as a midwife?'

Jashoda realized the justice of these words and said, with tears in her eyes, 'You are husband, you are guru. If I forget and say no, correct me. Where after all is the pain? Didn't Mistress-Mother breed thirteen? Does it hurt a tree to bear fruit?'

So this rule held. Kangalicharan became a professional father. Jashoda was by *profession* Mother. In fact to look at Jashoda now even the sceptic is convinced of the profundity of that song of the path of devotion. The song is as follows:

> Is a Mother so cheaply made?
> Not just by dropping a babe!

Around the paved courtyard on the ground floor of the Haldar house over a dozen auspicious milch cows live in some state in large rooms. Two Biharis look after them as Mother Cows. There are mountains of rind-bran-hay-grass-molasses. Mrs Haldar believes that the more the cow eats, the more milk she gives. Jashoda's place in the house is now above the Mother Cows. The Mistress's sons become incarnate Brahma and create progeny. Jashoda preserves the progeny.

Mrs Haldar kept a strict watch on the free flow of her supply of milk. She called Kangalicharan to her presence and said, 'Now then, my Brahmin son? You used to stir the vat at the shop, now take up the cooking at home and give her a rest. Two of her own, three here, how can she cook at day's end after suckling five?'

Kangalicharan's intellectual eye was thus opened. Downstairs the two Biharis gave him a bit of chewing tobacco and said, 'Mistress Mother said right. We serve the Cow Mother as well—your woman is the Mother of the world.'

From now on Kangalicharan took charge of the cooking at home. Made the children his assistants. Gradually he became an expert in cooking plantain curry, lentil soup, and pickled fish, and by constantly feeding Nabin a head-curry with the head of the goat dedicated to the Lionseated he tamed that ferocious cannabis-artist and drunkard. As a result Nabin inserted Kangali into the temple of Shiva the King. Jashoda, eating well-prepared rice and curry every day, became as inflated as the *bank account* of a Public Works Department *officer.* In addition, Mistress-Mother gave her milk gratis. When Jashoda became pregnant, she would send her preserves, conserves, hot and sweet balls.

Thus even the sceptics were persuaded that the Lionseated had appeared to Jashoda as a midwife for this very reason. Otherwise who has ever heard or seen such things as constant pregnancies, giving birth, giving milk like a cow, without a thought, to others' children? Nabin too lost his bad thoughts. Devotional feelings came to him by themselves. Whenever he saw Jashoda he called out 'Mother! Mother! Dear Mother!' Faith in the greatness of the Lionseated was rekindled in the area and in the air of the neighbourhood blew the *electrifying* influence of goddess-glory.

Everyone's devotion to Jashoda became so strong that at weddings,showers, namings,and sacred-threadings they invited her and gave her the position of chief fruitful woman. They looked with a comparable eye on Nepal-Gopal-Neno-Boncha-Patal etc. because they were Jashoda's children, and as each grew up, he got a sacred thread and started catching pilgrims for the temple. Kangali did not have to find husbands for Radharani, Altarani, Padmarani and such daughters. Nabin found them husbands with exemplary dispatch and the faithful mother's faithful daughters went off each to run the household of her own Shiva! Jashoda's worth went up in the Haldar house. The husbands are pleased because the wives' knees no longer knock when they riffle the almanac. Since their childern are being reared on Jashoda's milk, they can be the Holy Child in bed at will. The wives no longer have an excuse to say 'no'. The wives are happy. They can keep their figures. They can wear blouses and bras of 'European cut'. After keeping the fast of Shiva's night by watching all-night picture shows they are no longer obliged to breast-feed their babies. All this was possible because of Jashoda. As a result Jashoda became vocal and, constantly suckling the infants, she opined as she sat in the Mistress's room, 'A woman breeds, so here medicine, there blood-peshur, here doctor's visits. Showoffs! Look at me! I've become a year-breeder! So is my body failing, or is my milk drying? Makes your skin crawl? I hear they are drying their milk with injishuns.[4] Never heard of such things!'

The fathers and uncles of the current young men of the Haladar house used to whistle at the maidservants as soon as hair grew on their upper lips. The young ones were reared by the Milk-Mother's milk, so they looked upon the maid and the cook, their Milk-Mother's friends, as mothers too and started walking around the girls' school. The maids said, 'Joshi! You came as The Goddess! You made the air of this house change!' So one day as the youngest son was squatting to watch Jashoda's milking, she said, 'There dear, my Lucky! All this because you swiped him in the leg! Whose wish was it then?' 'The Lionseated's,' said Haldar junior.

He wanted to know how Kangalicharan could be Brahma without feet? This encroached on divine area, and he forgot the question.

All is the Lionseated's will!

3

Kangali's shins were cut in the fifties, and our narrative has reached the present. In twenty-five years, sorry, in thirty, Jashoda has been confined twenty times. The maternities toward the end were profitless, for a new wind entered the Haldar house somehow. Let's finish the business of the twenty-five or thirty years. At the beginning of the narrative Jashoda was the mother of three sons. Then she became gravid seventeen times. Mrs Haldar died. She dearly wished that one of her daughters-in-law should have the same good fortune as her mother-in-law. In the family the custom was to have a second wedding if a couple could produce twenty children. But the daughters-in-law called a halt at twelve-thirteen-fourteen. By evil counsel they were able to explain to their husbands and make arrangements at the hospital. All this was the bad result of the new wind. Wise men have never allowed a new wind to enter the house. I've heard from my grandmother that a certain gentleman would come to her house to read the liberal journal *Saturday Letter.* He would never let the tome enter his home. 'The moment wife, or mother, or sister reads that paper,' he would say, 'she'll say "I'm a woman! Not a mother, not a sister not a wife."' If asked what the result would be, he'd say, 'They would wear shoes while they cooked.' It is a perennial rule that the power of the new wind disturbs the peace of the women's quarter.

It was always the sixteenth century in the Haldar household. But at the sudden significant rise in the membership of the house the sons started building new houses and splitting. The most objectionable thing was that in the matter of motherhood, the old lady's granddaughters-in-law had breathed a completely different air before they crossed her threshold. In vain did the Mistress say that there was plenty of money, plenty to eat. The old man had dreamed of filling half Calcutta with Haldars. The granddaughters-in-law were unwilling. Defying the old lady's tongue, they took off to their husbands' places of work. At about this time, the pilgrim-guides of the Lionseated had a tremendous fight and some unknown person or persons turned the image of the goddess around. The Mistress's heart broke at the thought that the Mother had turned her back. In pain she ate an unreasonable quantity of jackfruit in full summer and died shitting and vomiting.

4

Death liberated the Mistress, but the sting of staying alive is worse than death.

Jashoda was genuinely sorry at the Mistress's death. When an elderly person dies in the neighbourhood, it's Basini who can weep most elaborately. She is an old maidservant of the house. But Jashoda's meal ticket was offered up with the Mistress. She astounded everyone by weeping even more elaborately.

'Oh blessed Mother!' Basini wept. 'Widowed, when you lost your crown, you became the Master and protected everyone! Whose sins sent you away Mother! Ma, when I said, don't eat so much jackfruit, you didn't listen to me at all Mother!'

Jashoda let Basini get her breath and lamented in that pause, 'Why should you stay, Mother! You are blessed, why should you stay in this sinful world! The daughters-in-law have moved the throne! When the tree says I won't bear, alas it's a sin! Could you bear so much sin, Mother! Then did the Lionseated turn her back, Mother! You knew the abode of good works had become the abode of sin, it was not for you Mother! Your heart left when the Master left Mother! You held your body only because you thought of the family. O mistresses, O daughters-in-law! take a vermillion print of her footstep! Fortune will be tied to the door if you keep that print! If you touch your forehead to it every morning, pain and disease will stay out!'

Jashoda walked weeping behind the corpse to the burning ghat and said on return, 'I saw with my own eyes a chariot descend from heaven, take Mistress Mother from the pyre, and go on up.'

After the funeral days were over, the eldest daughter-in-law said to Jashoda, 'Brahmin sister! the family is breaking up. Second and Third are moving to the house in Beleghata. Fourth and Fifth are departing to Maniktala-Bagmari. Youngest will depart to our Dakshineswar house.'

'Who stays here?'

'I will. But I'll let the downstairs. Now must the family be folded up. You reared everyone on your milk, food was sent every day. The last child was weaned, still

Mother sent you food for eight years. She did what pleased her. Her children said nothing. But it's no longer possible.'

'What'll happen to me, elder daughter-in-law-sister?'

'If you cook for my household, your board is taken care of. But what'll you do with yours?'

'What?'

'It's for you to say. You are the mother of twelve living children! The daughters are married. I hear the sons call pilgrims, eat temple food, stretch out in the courtyard. Your Brahmin-husband has set himself up in the Shiva temple, I hear. What do you need?'

Jashoda wiped her eyes. 'Well! Let me speak to the Brahmin.'

Kangalicharan's temple had really caught on. 'What will you do in my temple?' he asked.

'What does Nabin's niece do?'

'She looks after the temple household and cooks. You haven't been cooking at home for a long time. Will you be able to push the temple traffic?'

'No meals from the big house. Did that enter your thieving head? What'll you eat?'

'You don't have to worry,' said Nabin.

'Why did I have worry for so long? You're bringing it in at the temple, aren't you? You've saved everything and eaten the food that sucked my body.'

'Who sat and cooked?'

'The man brings, the woman cooks and serves. My lot is inside out. Then you ate my food, now you'll give me food. Fair's fair. '

Kangali said on the beat, 'Where did you bring in the food? Could you have gotten the Haldar house? Their door opened for *you* because *my* legs were cut off.

The Master had wanted to set *me* up in business. Forgotten everything, you cunt?'

'Who's the cunt, you or me? Living off a wife's carcass, you call that a man?'

The two fought tooth and nail and cursed each other to the death. Finally Kangali said, 'I don't want to see your face again. Buzz off!'

'All right.'

Jashoda too left angry. In the mean time the various pilgrim-guide factions conspired to turn the image's face forward, otherwise disaster was imminent. As a result, penance rituals were being celebrated with great ceremony at the temple. Jashoda went to throw herself at the goddess's feet. Her aging, milkless, capacious breasts are breaking in pain. Let the Lionseated understand her pain and tell her the way.

Jashoda lay three days in the courtyard. Perhaps the Lionseated has also breathed the new wind. She did not appear in a dream. Moreover, when, after her three days' fast, Jashoda went back shaking to her place, her youngest came by. 'Dad will stay at the temple. He's told Naba and I to ring the bells. We'll get money and holy food every day.'

'I see! Where's dad?'

'Lying down. Golapi-auntie is scratching the prickly heat on his back. Asked us to buy candy with some money. So we came to tell you.'

Jashoda understood that her usefulness had ended not only in the Haldar house but also for Kangali. She broke her fast in name and went to Nabin to complain. It was Nabin who dragged the Lionseated's image the other way. After he had settled the dispute with the other pilgrim-guides re the overhead income from the goddess Basanti ritual, the goddess Jagadhatri ritual, and the autumn Durga Puja, it was he who once again pushed and pulled the image the right way. He'd poured some liquor into his aching throat, had smoked a bit of cannabis, and was now addressing the local electoral candidate: 'No offerings for the Mother from you! Her glory is back. Now we'll see how you win!'

Nabin is the proof of all the miracles that can happen if, even in this decade, one stays under the temple's power. He had turned the goddess's head himself and had himself believed that the Mother was averse because the pilgrim-guides were not organizing like all the want-votes groups. Now, after he had turned the goddess's head he had the idea that the Mother had turned on her own.

Jashoda said, 'What are you babbling?'

Nabin said, 'I'm speaking of mother's glory.'

Jashoda said, 'You think I don't know that you turned the image's head yourself?'

Nabin said, 'Shut up, Joshi God gave me ability, and intelligence, and only then could the thing be done through me.'

'Mother's glory has disappeared when you put your hands on her.'

'Glory disappeared! If so, how come, the fan is turning, and you are sitting under the fan? Was there ever an elettiri[5] fan on the porch ceiling?'

'I accept. But tell me, why did you burn my luck? What did I ever do to you?'

'Why? Kangali isn't dead.'

'Why wait for death? He's more than dead to me.'

'What's up?'

Jashoda wiped her eyes and said in a heavy voice,

'I've carried so many, I was the regular milk-mother at the Master's house. You know everything. I've never left the straight and narrow.'

'But of course. You are a portion of the Mother.'

'But Mother remains in divine fulfillment. Her 'portion' is about to die for want of food. Haldar-house has lifted its hand from me.'

'Why did you have to fight with Kangali? Can a man bear to be insulted on grounds of being supported?'

'Why did you have to plant your niece there?'

'That was divine play. Golapi used to throw herself in the temple. Little by little Kangali came to understand that he was the god's companion-incarnate and she *his* companion.'

'Companion indeed! I can get my husbend from her clutches with one blow of a broom!'

Nabin said, 'No! that can't be any more. Kangali is a man in his prime, how can he be pleased with you any more? Besides, Golapi's brother is a real hoodlum, and he is guarding her. Asked *me* to *get out.* If I smoke ten pipes, he smokes twenty. Kicked me in the midriff. I went to speak for you. Kangali said, don't talk to me about her. Doesn't know her man, knows her master's house. The master's house is her household god, let her go there.'

'I will.'

Then Jashoda returned home, half-crazed by the injustice of the world. But her heart couldn't abide the empty room. Whether it suckled or not, it's hard to sleep without a child at the breast. Motherhood is a great addiction. The addiction doesn't break even when the milk is dry. Forlorn Jashoda went to the Haldaress. She said, 'I'll cook and serve, if you want to pay me, if not, not. You must let me stay here. That sonofabitch is living at the temple. What disloyal sons! They are stuck there too. For whom shall I hold my room?'

'So stay. You suckled the children, and you're a Brahmin. So stay. But sister, it'll be hard for you. You'll stay in Basini's room with the others. You mustn't fight with anyone. The master is not in a good mood. His temper is rotten because his third son went to Bombay and married a local girl. He'll be angry if there's noise.'

Jashoda's good fortune was her ability to bear children. All this misfortune happened to her as soon as that vanished. Now is the downward time for Jashoda the milk-filled faithful wife who was the object of the reverence of the local houses devoted to the Holy Mother. It is human nature to feel an inappropriate vanity as one rises, yet not to feel the *surrender* of 'let me learn to bite the dust since I'm down' as one falls. As a result one makes demands for worthless things in the old way and gets kicked by the weak.

The same thing happened to Jashoda. Basini's crowd used to wash her feet and drink the water. Now Basini said easily, 'You'll wash your own dishes. Are you my master, that I'll wash your dishes. You are the master's servant as much as I am.'

As Jashoda roared, 'Do you know who I am?'she heard the eldest daughter-in-law scold, 'This is what I feared. Mother gave her a swelled head. Look here, Brahmin sister! I didn't call you, you begged to stay, don't break the peace.'

Jashoda understood that now no one would attend to a word she said. She cooked and served in silence and in the late afternoon she went to the temple porch and started to weep. She couldn't even have a good cry.

She heard the music for the evening worship at the temple of Shiva. She wiped her eyes and got up. She said to herself, 'Now save me, Mother! Must I finally sit by the roadside with a tin cup? Is that what you want?'

The days would have passed in cooking at the Haldar-house and complaining to the Mother. But that was not enough for Jashoda. Jashoda's body seemed to keel over. Jashoda doesn't understand why nothing pleases her. Everything seems confused inside her head. When she sits down to cook she thinks she's the milk-mother of this house. She's going home in a showy sari with a free meal in her hand. Her breasts feel empty, as if wasted. She had never thought she wouldn't have a child's mouth at her nipple.

Joshi became bemused. She serves nearly all the rice and curry, but forgets to eat. Sometimes she speaks to Shiva the King, 'If Mother can't do it, you take me away. I can't pull any more.'

Finally it was the sons of the eldest daughter-in-law who said, 'Mother! Is the milk-Mother sick? She acts strange.'

The eldest daughter-in-law said, 'Let's see.'

The eldest son said, 'Look here! She's a Brahmin's daughter, if anything happens to her, it'll be a sin for us.'

The daughter-in-law went to ask. Jashoda had started the rice and then lain down in the kitchen on the spread edge of her sari. The eldest daughter-in-law, looking at her bare body, said, 'Brahmin sister! Why does the top of your left tit look so red? God! flaming red!'

'Who knows? It's like a stone pushing inside. Very hard, like a rock.'

'What is it?'

'Who knows? I suckled so many, perhaps that's why?'

'Nonsense! One gets breast-stones or pus-in-the-tit if there's milk. Your youngest is ten.'

'That one is gone. The one before survived. That one died at birth. Just as well. This sinful world!'

'Well the doctor comes tomorrow to look at my grandson. I'll ask. Doesn't look good to me.'

Jashoda said with her eyes closed, 'Like a stone tit, with a stone inside. At first the hard ball moved about, now it doesn't move, doesn't budge.'

'Let's show the doctor.'

'No, sister daughter-in-law, I can't show my body to a male doctor.'

At night when the doctor came the eldest daughter-in-law asked him in her son's presence. She said, 'No pain, no burning, but she is keeling over.'

The doctor said, 'Go ask if the *nipple* has shrunk, if the armpit is swollen like a seed.'

Hearing 'swollen like a seed,' the eldest daughter-in-law thought, 'How crude!' Then she did her field investigations and said, 'She says all that you've said has been happening for some time.'

'How old?'

'If you take the eldest son's age she'll be about fifty-five.'

The doctor said, 'I'll give you medicine.'

Going out, he said to the eldest son, 'I hear your *cook* has a problem with her *breast.* I think you should take her to the *cancer hospital.* I didn't see her. But from what I heard it could be *cancer* of the *mammary gland.*'

Only the other day the eldest son lived in the

sixteenth century. He has arrived at the twentieth century very recently. Of his thirteen offspring he has arranged the marriages of the daughters, and the sons have grown up and are growing up at their own speed and in their own way. But even now his grey cells are covered in the darkness of the eighteenth- and the pre-Bengal-Renaissance nineteenth centuries. He still does not take smallpox vaccination and says, 'Only the lower classes get smallpox. I don't need to be vaccinated. An upper-caste family, respectful of gods and Brahmins, does not contract that disease.'

He pooh-poohed the idea of cancer and said, 'Yah! Cancer indeed! That easy! You misheard, all she needs is an ointment. I can't send a Brahmin's daughter to a hospital just on your word.'

Jashoda herself also said, 'I can't go to hospital. Ask me to croak instead. I didn't go to hospital to breed, and I'll go now? That corpse-burning devil returned a cripple because he went to hospital!'

The elder daughter-in-law said, 'I'll get you a herbal ointment. This ointment will surely soothe. The hidden boil will show its tip and burst.'

The herbal ointment was a complete failure. Slowly Jashoda gave up eating and lost her strength. She couldn't keep her sari on the left side. Sometimes she felt burning, sometimes pain. Finally the skin broke in many places and sores appeared. Jashoda took to her bed.

Seeing the hang of it, the eldest son was afraid, if at his house a Brahmin died! He called Jashoda's sons and spoke to them harshy, 'It's your mother, she fed you so long, and now she is about to die! Take her with you! She has everyone and she should die in a Kayastha[4] household?'

Kangali cried a lot when he heard this story. He came to Jashoda's almost-dark room and said, 'Wife! You are a blessed auspicious faithful woman! After I spurned you, within two years the temple dishes were stolen, I suffered from boils in my back, and that snake Golapi tricked Napla, broke the safe, stole everything and opened a shop in Tarakeswar. Come, I'll keep you in state.'

Jashoda said, 'Light the lamp.'

Kangali lit the lamp.

Jashoda showed him her bare left breast, thick with running sores and said, 'See these sores? Do you know how these sores smell? What will you do with me now? Why did you come to take me?'

'The Master called.'

'Then the master doesn't want to keep me.' Jashoda sighed and said, 'There is no solution about me. What can you do with me?'

'Whatever, I'll take you tomorrow. Today I clean the room. Tomorrow for sure.'

'Are the boys well? Noblay and Gaur used to come, they too have stopped.'

'All the bastards are selfish. Sons of my spunk after all. As inhuman as I.'

'You'll come tomorrow?'

'Yes—yes—yes.'

Jashoda smiled suddenly. A heart-splitting nostalgia-provoking smile.

Jashoda said, 'Dear, remember?'

'What, wife?'

'How you played with these tits? You couldn't sleep otherwise? My lap was never empty, if this one left my nipple, there was that one, and then the boys of the Master's house. How I could, I wonder now!'

'I remember everything, wife!'

In this instant Kangali's words are true. Seeing Jashoda's broken, thin, suffering form even Kangali's selfish body and instincts and belly-centred consciousness remembered the past and suffered some empathy. He held Jashoda's hand and said, 'You have fever?'

'I get feverish all the time. I think by the strength of the sores.'

'Where does this rotten stink come from?'

'From these sores.'

Jashoda spoke with her eyes closed. Then she said, 'Bring the holy doctor. He cured Gopal's *typhoid* with *homoeopathy*.'

'I'll call him. I'll take you tomorrow.'

Kangali left. That he went out, the tapping of his crutches, Jashoda couldn't hear. With her eyes shut, with the idea that Kangali was in the room, she said spiritlessly, 'If you suckle you're a mother, all lies! Nepal and Gopal don't look at me, and the Master's boys don't spare a peek to ask how I'm doing.' The sores on her breast kept mocking her with a hundred mouths, a hundred eyes. Jashoda opened her eyes and said, 'Do you hear?'

Then she realized that Kangali had left.

In the night she sent Basini for *Lifebuoy* soap and at dawn she went to take a bath with the soap. Stink, what a stink! If the body of a dead cat or dog rots in the garbage you can get a smell like this. Jashoda had forever scrubbed her breasts carefully with soap and oil, for the master's sons had put the nipples in their mouth. Why did those breasts betray her in the end? Her skin burns with the sting of soap. Still Jashoda washed herself with soap. Her head was ringing, everything seemed dark. There was fire in Jashoda's body, in her head. The black floor was very cool. Jashoda spread her sari and lay down. She could not bear the weight of her breast standing up.

As Jashoda lay down, she lost sense and consciousness with fever. Kangali came at the proper time: but seeing Jashoda he lost his grip. Finally Nabin came and rasped, 'Are these people human? She reared all the boys with her milk and they don't call a doctor? I'll call Hari the doctor.'

Haribabu took one look at her and said, 'Hospital.'

Hospitals don't admit people who are so sick. At the efforts and recommendations of the elder son, Jashoda was admitted.

'What's the matter? O Doctorbabu, what's the problem?' Kangali asked, weeping like a boy.

'Cancer.'

'You can get cancer in a tit?'

'Otherwise how did she get it?'

'Her own twenty, thirty boys at the master's house—she had a lot of milk—'

'What did you say? How many did she *feed*?'

'About fifty for sure.'

'Fif-ty!'

'Yes sir.'

'She had twenty childern?'

'Yes sir.'

'*God*!'

'Sir!'

'What?'

'Is it because she suckled so many—?'

'One can't say why someone gets cancer, one can't say. But when people breast-feed too much—didn't you realize earlier? It didn't get to this in a day.'

'She wasn't with me, sir. We quarrelled—'

'I see.'

'How do you see her? Will she get well?'

'Get well! See how long she lasts. You've brought her in the last stages. No one survives this stage.'

Kangali left weeping. In the late afternoon, harassed by Kangali's lamentations, the eldest son's second son went to the doctor. He was minimally anxious about Jashoda —but his father nagged him and he was financially dependent on his father.

The doctor explained everything to him. It happened not in a day, but over a long time. Why? No one could tell. How does one perceive breast cancer? A hard lump inside the breast toward the top can be removed. Then gradually the lump inside becomes large, hard and like a congealed pressure. The skin is expected to turn orange, as is expected a shrinking of the nipple. The gland in the armpit can be inflamed. When there is *ulceration*, that is to say sores, one can call it the final stages. Fever? From the point of view of seriousness it falls in the second or third category. If there is something like a sore in the body, there can be fever. This is *secondary*.

The second son was confused with all this specialist talk. He said, 'Will she live?'

'No.'

'How long will she suffer?'

'I don't think too long.'

'When there's nothing to be done, how will you

treat her?'

'*Painkiller, sedative, antibiotic* for the fever. Her body is very, very *down*.'

'She stopped eating.'

'You didn't take her to a doctor?'

'Yes."

'Didn't he tell you?'

'Yes.'

'What did he say?'

'That it might be cancer. Asked us to take her to the hospital. She didn't agree.'

'Why would she? She'd die!'

The second son came home and said, 'When Arun-doctor said she had *cancer*, she might have survived if treated then.'

His mother said, 'If you know that much then why didn't take you her? Did I stop you?'

Somewhere in the minds of the second son and his mother an unknown sense of guilt and remorse came up like bubbles in the dirty and stagnant water and vanished instantly.

Guilt said—she lived with us, we never took a look at her, when did the disease catch her, we didn't take it seriously at all. She was a silly person, reared so many of us, we didn't look after her. Now, with everyone around her she's dying in hospital, so many children, husband living, when she clung to us, then we had—! What an alive body she had, milk leaped out of her, we never thought she would have this disease.

The disappearance of guilt said—who can undo Fate? It was written that she'd die of *cancer*—who'd stop it? It would have been wrong if she had died here—her husband and sons would have asked, how did she die?

We have been saved from that wrongdoing. No one can say anything.

The eldest son assured them, 'Now Arun-doctor says no one survives *cancer.* The *cancer* that Brahmin-sister has can lead to cutting of the tit, removing the uterus, even after that people die of *cancer.* See, Father gave us a lot of reverence toward Brahmins—we are alive by father's grace. If Brahmin-sister had died in our house, we would have had to perform the penance-ritual.'

Patients much less sick than Jashoda die much sooner. Jashoda astonished the doctors by hanging on for about a month in hospital. At first Kangali, Nabin, and the boys did indeed come and go, but Jashoda remained the same, comatose, cooking with fever, spellbound. The sores on her breast gaped more and more and the breast now looks like an open wound. It is covered by a piece of thin *gauze* soaked in *antiseptic lotion*, but the sharp smell of putrefying flesh is circulating silently in the room's air like incense-smoke. This brought an ebb in the enthusiasm of Kangali and the other visitors. The doctor said as well, 'Is she not responding? All for the better. It's hard to bear without consciousness, can anyone bear such death-throes consciously?'

'Does she know that we come and go?'

'Hard to say.'

'Does she eat.'

'Through tubes.'

'Do people live this way?'

'Now you're very—'

The doctor understood that he was unreasonably angry because Jashoda was in this condition. He was angry with Jashoda, with Kangali, with women who don't take the signs of breast-cancer *seriously* enough and finally die in this dreadful and hellish pain. Cancer constantly defeats patient and doctor. One patient's cancer means the patient's death and the defeat of science, and of course of the doctor. One can medicate against the secondary symptom, if eating stops one can *drip glucose* and feed the body, if the lungs become incapable of breathing there is *oxygen*—but the advance of *cancer*, its expansion, spread, and killing, remain unchecked. The word *cancer* is a general signifier, by which in the different parts of the body is meant different *malignant growths.* Its characteristic properties are to destroy the infected area of the body, to spread by *metastasis,* to return after *removal,* to creat *toxaemia.*

Kangali came out without a proper answer to his question. Returning to the temple, he said to Nabin and his sons, 'There's no use going any more. She doesn't know us, doesn't open her eyes, doesn't realize anything. The doctor is doing what he can.'

Nabin said, 'If she dies?'

'They have the *telephone number* of the old Master's eldest son, they'll call.'

'Suppose she wants to see you. Kangali, your wife is a blessed auspicious faithful woman! Who would say the mother of so many. To see her body—but she didn't bend, didn't look elsewhere.'

Talking thus, Nabin became gloomily silent. In fact, since he'd seen Jashoda's infested breasts, many a philosophic thought and sexological argument have been slowly circling Nabin's drug-and-booze-addled dim head like great rutting snakes emptied of venom. For example, I lusted after her? This is the end of that intoxicating bosom? Ho! Man's body's a zero. To be crazy for that is to be crazy.

Kangali didn't like all this talk. His mind had already *rejected* Jashoda. When he saw Jashoda in the Haldar-house he was truly affected and even after her admission into hospital he was passionately anxious. But now that feeling is growing cold. The moment the doctor said Jashoda wouldn't last, he put her out of mind almost painlessly. His sons are his sons. Their mother had become a distant person for a long time. Mother meant hair in a huge topknot, blindingly white clothes, a strong personality. The person lying in the hospital is someone else, not Mother.

Breast *cancer* makes the brain *comatose*, this was a solution for Jashoda.

Jashoda understood that she had come to hospital, she was in the hospital, and that this desensitizing sleep was a medicated sleep. In her weak, infected, dazed brain she thought, has some son of the Haldar-house become a doctor?

No doubt he sucked her milk and is now repaying the milk-debt? But those boys entered the family business as soon as they left high school! However, why don't the people who are helping her so much free her from the stinking presence of her chest? What a smell, what treachery? Knowing these breasts to be the rice-winner, she had constantly conceived to keep them filled with milk. The breast's job is to hold milk. She kept her breast clean with perfumed soap, she never wore a top, even in youth, because her breasts were so heavy.

When the *sedation* lessens, Jashoda screams, 'Ah! Ah! Ah!'—and looks for the nurse and the doctor with passionate bloodshot eyes. When the doctor comes, she mutters with hurt feelings, 'You grew so big on my milk, and now you're hurting me so?

The doctor says, 'She sees her milk-sons all over the world.'

Again injection and sleepy numbness. Pain, tremendous pain, the cancer is spreading *at the expense of the human host.* Gradually Jashoda's left breast bursts and becomes like the *crater* of a volcano. The smell of putrefaction makes approach difficult.

Finally one night, Jashoda understood that her feet and hands were getting cold. She understood that death was coming. Jashoda couldn't open her eyes, but she understood that some people were looking at her hand. A needle pricked her arm. Painful breathing inside. Has to be. Who is looking? Are these her own people? The people whom she suckled because she carried them, or those she suckled for a living? Jashoda thought, after all, she had suckled the world, could she then die alone? The doctor who sees her every day, the person who will cover her face with a sheet, will put her on a cart, will lower her at the burning ghat, the untouchable who will put her in the furnace, are all her milk-sons. One must become Jashoda[7] if one suckles the world. One has to die friendless, with no one left to put a bit of water in the mouth. Yet someone was supposed to be there at the end. Who was it? It was who? Who was it?

Jashoda died at 11 p.m.

The Haldar-house was called on the phone. The phone didn't ring. The Haldars *disconnected* their phone at night.

Jashoda Devi, Hindu female, lay in the hospital morgue in the usual way, went to the burning ghat in a van, and was burnt. She was cremated by an untouchable.

Jashoda was God manifest, others do and did whatever she thought. Jashoda's death was also the death of God. When a mortal masquerades as God here below, she is forsaken by all and she must always die alone.

1987

Notes

1. Underclass Bengali pronunciation for 'crutches'

2. Actresses who have stereotyped the role of the self-sacrificing, long-suffering Indian wife and mother in commercial Hindi cinema.

3. Caste-Hindu widows become vegetarians in West Bengal as a sign of lifelong mourning.

4. Underclass Bengali prounciation for ' blood pressure' and ' injections.'

5. Underclass Bengali pronunciation for 'electric.'

6. Second caste in rank, immediately below the Brahmin.

7. The mythic mother of Krishna and in that sense the suckler of the world.

'breast-giver': for author, reader, teacher, subaltern, historian . . .[1]

gayatri chakravorty spivak

THAT HISTORY DEALS WITH REAL EVENTS and literature with imagined ones may now be seen as a difference in degree rather than in kind. The difference between cases of historical and literary events will always be there as a differential moment in terms of what is called 'the effect of the real'.[2] What is called history will always seem more real to us than what is called literature. Our very uses of the two separate words guarantees that.[3] This difference can never be exhaustively systematized. In fact, the ways in which the difference is articulated also has a hidden agenda. The historians' resistance to fiction relates to the fact that the writing of history and of literature has a social connotation even when these activities do not resemble what we understand by them today; and that historiography and literary pedagogy are disciplines.

Mahasweta Devi's own relationship to historical discourse seems clear. She has always been gripped by the individual in history. *Hajar Churashir Ma* (1973-74) in spite of its bold message, still belongs to the style of mainstream fiction. To this reader it seems as if the vision of *Hajar Churashir Ma*—the bringing-to-crisis of the personal through a political event of immediate magnitude (the 'climactic phase of the annihilation of the urban naxalites') pushed Mahasweta from what was perceived as 'literary' or 'subjective' into an experiment with a form perceived as 'historical.'[4] The stories of *Agnigarbha* (collected in 1978) mark the site of this difficult move. In *Aranyer Adhikar* (1977) the prose is beginning to bend into full-fledged 'historical fiction,' history imagined into fiction. The division between fact (historical event) and fiction (literary event) is operative in all these moves. Indeed, her repeated claim to legitimacy is that she researches thoroughly everything she represents in fiction.

Fiction of this sort relies for its effect on its 'effect of the real.' The plausibility of a Jashoda ('Stanadayini'or 'Breast-Giver'), a Draupadi ('Draupadi'), a Birsa Munda (*Aranyer Adhikar*) is that they could have existed as subalterns in a specific historical moment imagined and tested by orthodox assumptions. When the subalternist historian imagines a historical moment, within which shadowy named characters, backed up by some counter-insurgent or dominant-gender textual material, have their plausible being, in order that a historical narrative can coherently take shape, the assumptions are not very different. Those who read or write literature can claim as little of subaltern status as those who read or write history. The difference is that the subaltern as object is supposed to be imagined in one case and real in another. I am suggesting that it is a bit of both in both cases. The writer acknowledges this by claiming to do research (my fiction is also historical). The historian might acknowledge this by looking at the mechanics of representation (my history is also fictive). It is with this suggestion that I submit the following pages. My brief is very different from saying that history is only literature.

The Author's Own Reading: A Subject Position

By Mahasweta Devi's own account, 'Stanadayini' is a parable of India after decolonization.[5] Like the protagonist Jashoda, India is a mother-by-hire. All classes of people, the post-war rich, the ideologues, the indigenous bureaucracy, the diasporics, the people who are sworn to protect the new state, abuse and exploit her. If nothing is done to sustain her, nothing given back to her, and if scientific help comes too late, she will die of a consuming cancer. I suppose if one extended this parable the end of the story might come to 'mean' something like this: the ideological construct 'India' is too deeply informed by the goddess-infested reverse sexism of the Hindu majority. As long as there is this hegemonic cultural self-representation of India as a goddess-mother (dissimulating the possibility that this mother is a slave), she will collapse under the burden of the immense expectations that such a self-representation permits.

This interesting reading is not very useful from the perspective of a study of the subaltern. Here the representation of India is by way of the subaltern as metaphor. By the rules of a parable the logic of the connection between the tenor and vehicle of the metaphor must be made absolutely explicit.[6] Under the imperatives of such a reading, the 'effect of the real' of the vehicle must necessarily be underplayed. The subaltern must be seen only as the vehicle of a greater meaning. The traffic between the historian and the writer that I have been proposing could not be justified if one devoted oneself to this reading. In order that Mahasweta's parable be disclosed, what must be excluded from the story is precisely the attempt to represent the subaltern as such. I will therefore take the risk of putting to one side that all too neat reading, and unravel the text to pick up the threads of the excluded attempt.

This takes me to a general argument implicit within the study of the subaltern in the context of decolonization: if the story of the rise of nationalist resistance to imperialism is to be disclosed coherently, it is the role of the indigenous subaltern that must be strategically excluded. Then it can be argued that, in the initial stages of the consolidation of territorial imperialism, no organized political resistance was forthcoming. Through access to the cultural aspects of imperialism, the colonized countries acceded to sentiments of nationhood. It was then that genuine anti-imperialist resistance developed.[7]

As in the case of the opposition between fact and fiction, there is a certain good sense in this. The exclusion that must operate in order to preserve that good sense are at least two-fold. First, if nationalism is the *only* discourse credited with emancipatory possibilities in the imperialist theatre, then one must ignore the innumerable subaltern examples of resistance throughout the imperialist and pre-imperialist centuries, often suppressed by those very forces of nationalism which would be instrumental in changing the geo-political conjuncture from territorial imperialism to neo-colonialism, and which seem particularly useless in current situations of struggle.[8] Secondly, if *only* the emancipatory possibilities of the culture of imperialism are taken into account, the distortions in the ideals of a national culture when imported into a colonial theatre would go unnoticed.[9]

Citizens of the nation must give something to the nation rather than merely take from it, the gist of Mahasweta's own reading of 'Stanadayini,' is one of the many slogans of a militant nationalism. It can accommodate sentiments extending from '*sat koti santanere he mugdha janani, rekhechho bangali kore manush karoni*' ['Fond mother, you have kept your seventy million children Bengalis but haven't made them human'—Tagore] to 'Ask not what your country can do for you' (John F Kennedy, Inaugural Address). In spite of the best possible personal politics, the reading Mahasweta Devi offers of her own story, entailing her subject-position as writer, signifies that narrative of nationalism that is perceived as a product of the culture of imperialism. This too obliges me to set it aside and to wonder what her text, as statement, articulates that must in its turn be set aside so that her reading can emerge.

The Teacher and Reader(s): More Subject-Positions

Mahasweta's text might show in many ways how the narratives of nationalism have been and remain irrelevant to the life of the subordinate. The elite culture of nationalism participated and participates with the colonizer in various ways.[10] In Mahasweta's story we see the detritus of that participation. In a certain sense, we witness there the ruins of the ideas of parliamentary democracy and of the nation when bequeathed to the elite of a colonized people outside the supposedly 'natural' soil of the production of those ideas. Some of us would speculate that, used as a teaching tool (from within the subject-position of the teacher in a certain discursive formation), stories such as this can deconstruct those ideas even in their so-called natural habitat. It is for us important that, in 'Stanadayini,' the piece of flotsam least susceptible to those ideas is the subaltern as gendered subject, a subject-position different from the subaltern as class-subject. In orthodox literary-critical circles, the authority of the author's reading still holds a certain glamour. By way of Foucault, I have therefore taken some pains to explain why I focus on the subaltern as gendered subject rather than as an allegorical seme for Mother India.

If 'the need to make the subaltern classes the subject of their own history [has among other] themes . . . provided a fresh critical thrust to much recent writing on modern Indian history and society,' then a text about the (im)possibility of 'making' the subaltern gender the subject of its own story seems to me to have a certain pertinence.[11] Toward the end of this essay, I will discuss the need to put the 'im' of 'impossible' in parentheses.

Accounts of history and literary pedagogy, as they appropriate and disseminate reports and tales, are two ways in which mind-sets are set.[12] The reading of 'Stanadayini' presented here, assigning the subject-position to the teacher/reader, can be helpful in combating a certain tendency in literary pedagogy that still shapes, by remote control, the elite in the most prestigious Indian educational institutions: the so-called radical teaching of literary criticism and literature in the United States and perhaps also in Britain.

This dominant *radical* reader in the Anglo-US reactively homogenizes the Third World and sees it only in the context of nationalism and ethnicity. The dominant reader in India who is resistant to such homogenization, and who is to be distinguished from students of reading theory in elite Indian institutions, inhabits a reading practice that is indistinguishable from the *orthodox* position in the Anglo-US. The Indian reader, a faceless person within the sphere of influence of a postcolonial humanistic education (I use this awkward terminology because sociologists, economists, doctors, scientists, et cetera are not outside of this sphere), takes this orthodox position to be the 'natural' way to read literature. The position is undergirded by the author's account of her 'original vision.' In this particular case, that account (the reading of the story as a parable) would forbid the fulfillment of another assumption implicit in the orthodox position, the psychologistic or characterological assumption that we 'feel' the story as if it is gossip about nonexistent people. The general reader can straddle such contradictions easily. The historians, anthropologists, sociologists, and doctors among them can know or show that any group's perception of the 'natural' meanings of things may be discursively constructed through an erring common sense. When, however, it comes to their own presuppositions about the 'natural' way to read literature, they cannot admit that this might be a construction as well, that this subject-position might also be assigned. Given that this way of reading has been in control for at least a couple of centuries in post-Enlightenment Europe, and has served to distinguish our indigenous elite from the uneducated, to read thus certainly engages our affects.[13] I will not enter the abstruse arguments about the historicity or phenomenality of affects.[14] Nor will I suggest that there is a correct way to train our affects. Indeed, it is not only 'false consciousness' that is 'ideological.' A Foucauldian or, in this case deconstructive position would oblige us to admit that 'truths' are constructions as well, and that we cannot avoid producing them.

Without venturing up to the perilous necessity of asking the question of true readings or true feelings, then, I will propose an alternative. Let us jealously guard the orthodoxy's right to be 'moved' by literature 'naturally,' and tremble before the author's authority. By a slightly different argument, let us consider 'literature' as a use of language where the transactional quality of reading is socially guaranteed. A literary text exists between writer and reader. This makes literature peculiarly susceptible to didactic use. When literature is used didactically, it is generally seen as a site for the deployment of 'themes,' even the theme of the undoing of thematicity, of unreadability, of undecidability.[15] This is not a particularly 'elite' approach, although it may be called 'unnatural.' On the one hand, Marxist literary criticism as well as a remark like Chinua Achebe's 'all art is propaganda, though not all propaganda is art' can be taken as cases of such a 'thematic'approach.[16] On the other hand, some 'elite' approaches (deconstructive, structuralist, semiotic, structuralist-psychoanalytic, phenomenological, discourse-theoretical; though not necessarily feminist, reader-responsist, intertextual, or linguistic) can also be accommodated here.

(Any reader nervous about the fact that Mahasweta Devi has probably not read much of the material critically illuminated by her text should stop here.)

(Elite) approaches: 'Stanadayini' in Marxist Feminism

An allegorical or parabolic reading of 'Stanadayini' such as Mahasweta's own would reduce the complexity of the signals put up by the text. Let us consider another reductive allegorical or parabolic reading. This reading can be uncovered in terms of a so-called Marxist-feminist thematics. Peculiar to the orthodoxy of US Marxist-feminism and some, though not all, British varieties, these thematics unfold in a broadly pre-Althusserian way.[17]

Here is a representative generalization: 'It is the provision by men of means of subsistence to women during the child-bearing period, and not the sex division of labour in itself, that forms the material basis for women's subordination in class society.'[18]

If one were teaching 'Stanadayini' as the site of a critical deployment of Marxist-feminist thematics, one would point out that the text reverses this generalization. The protagonist subaltern Jashoda, her husband crippled by the youngest son of a wealthy household, becomes a wet-nurse for them. Her repeated gestation and lactation support her husband and family. By the logic of the production of value, they are both means of production. By the logic of sexual reproduction, he is her means of production (though not owned by her) as the field-beast or the beast of burden is the slave's. In fact, even as it reverses the Marxist-feminist generalization I quote above, Jashoda's predicament also undoes, by placing within a gender-context, the famous Roman distinction, invoked by Marx, between *instrumentum vocale* ('the speaking tool'—Jashoda, the woman-wife-mother) and *instrumentum semi-vocale* (the working beast—Kangali, the man-husband-father).[19] This is worth noticing because one of the most important Marxist-feminist critiques of the labour theory of value is that it does not take sexual reproduction into account when speaking of social reproduction or the reproduction of labour-power.[20]

The political economy or the sexual division of labour changes considerably by the sale of Jashoda's labour-power, which is specific to the female of the species. One may even call this a moment of transition from one mode of social reproduction to another. Or perhaps one could call it the moment of the emergence of value and its immediate extraction and appropriation. These changes take place within extended domestic economy. One might therefore call it a transition from the domestic to the 'domestic.' 'Stanadayini' stalls the classic Engelsian-feminist narrative, which sees the family as the agent of transition from domestic to civil, private to public, home to work, sex to class. It should be pointed out that it also displaces the new

Marxist-feminist critique of such a position (which I quote below) by bringing back the focus on the mothering female: 'The identification of the family as the sole site of maintenance of labour power overstates its role at the level of immediate production. It fetishizes the family at the level of total social reproduction, by representing generational replacement as the only source of renewal of society's labour force.'[21]

The emergence of (exchange) value and its immediate appropriation in 'Stanadayini' may be thematized as follows:

The milk that is produced in one's own body for one's own children is a use-value. When there is a superfluity of use values, exchange values arise. That which cannot be used is exchanged. As soon as the (exchange) value of Jashoda's milk emerges, it is appropriated. Good food and constant sexual servicing are provided so that she can be kept in prime condition for optimum lactation. The milk she produces for her children is presumably through 'necessary labour.' The milk that she produces for the children of her master's family is through 'surplus labour.' Indeed, this is how the origin of this transition is described in the story: 'But today, hearing from his wife about Jashoda's *surplus* [in English in the original] milk, the second son said all of a sudden, 'Way found'.

In order to keep her in prime condition to produce surplus, the sexual division of labour is easily reversed. Her husband is relegated to housework. '"Now take up the cooking at home and give her a rest," says the Mistress. "Two of her own, three here, how can she cook at day's end after suckling five?"'. This particular parabolic or allegoric reading is not necessarily disqualified by the fact that Jashoda's body produces a surplus that is fully consumed by the owners of her labour-power and leads to no *capital* accumulation (as it would have if the milk had been bottled and sold in the open market at a profit), although rearing children is indirectly an 'investment in the future.' Like the economy of the temple (which will provide the husband a patriarchal escape route), this domestic/'domestic' transition survives in a relatively autonomous way in the pores of a comprador capitalism whose outlines are only shadowily indicated in Mahasweta's story. If within this pre-capitalist surplus-appropriation we assumed Jashoda's milk to be standing in for the 'universal equivalent' in the restricted 'domestic' sphere, we might get away with pronouncing that the situation is what Marx, with obviously unwitting irony, would describe as 'simple reproduction.'[22]

This account of the deployment of some Marxist-feminist 'themes' introduces a stutter in the pre-supposition that women's work is typically non-productive of value. I am not considering women's insertion into the labour-process. In that narrative woman is less than the norm of 'free labour.' I am half-fantasizing, rather, about an area where the product of a woman's body has been historically susceptible to idealization—just as, in the classical Marxian argument, the reason why the free (male) labourer becomes a 'proletarian' under capitalism is not that he has nothing but his body but that, his product, being a value-term, is susceptible to idealization. The commodity, by the same token, is susceptible to being transformed to commodity-capital.[23] Yet the word 'proletarian'—'one who serves the state with nothing but his [sic] offspring'

(OED)—continues to carry an effaced mark of sexuality. Am I then proposing to endorse some weird theory where labour-power is replaced by the power of gestation and lactation? Or am I suggesting that the study of this particular female activity, professional mothering, as it is to be found, for example, in Fanny Fay-Sallois's excellent *Les Nourrices à Paris aux XIX siècle*, be included in any study of the subaltern?[24]

I am suggesting both less and more. I see no particular reason to curtail the usefulness of classical Marxist analysis, within its own limits, by a tendentious requirement for uncritical inclusiveness. Any critique of strategic exclusions should bring analytical presuppositions to crisis. Marxism and feminism must become persistent interruptions of each other. The 'mode of existence' of literature, as of language, is where 'the task of understanding does not basically amount to *recognizing* the form used, but . . . to understanding its novelty and *not* to recognizing its identity . . . The understander, belonging to the same language community, is attuned to the linguistic form *not* as a fixed, self-identical signal, but as a changeable and adaptable sign . . . The ideal of mastering a language is absorption of signality by pure semioticity.'[25]

As the user, occupying different instituted 'I' -slots, understands the supposedly self-identical signal, always supposedly indicating the same thing, she persistently distances herself, in heterogeneous ways, from that monumentalized self-identity, the 'proper meaning.'[26] We can use 'Stanadayini,' a discursive literary production, from the perspective of Marxist-feminist thematics by considering how it helps us distance ourselves from two self-identical propositions that ground much of subalternist analysis implicitly:

a. that the free worker as such is male (hence the narrative of value-emergence and value-appropriation; the labour power specific to the female body is susceptible to the production of value in the strict sense);

b. that the *nature* of woman is physical, nurturing and affective (hence the professional-mother).

A good deal of feminist scholarship has reasonably and soberly analysed and revised these propositions in recent years.[27] I will consider two provocative examples at the end of this section. Such painstaking speculative scholarship, though invaluable to our collective enterprise does, however, *reason* gender into existing paradigms.[28] By contrast, emphasizing the literariness of literature, pedagogy invites us to take a distance from the continuing project of reason. Without this supplementary distancing, a position and its counter-position, both held in the discourse of reason, will keep legitimizing each other. Feminism and masculism, benevolent or militant, might not then be able to avoid becoming opposing faces of each other.[29]

Resuming, then, our fabulation with Marxist-feminist thematics on the occasion of 'Stanadayini' let us consider Jashoda's 'alienation' from her breasts:

> She thought of her breasts as most precious objects. At night when Kangalicharan started to give her a feel she said 'Look. I'm going to pull our weight with these. Take good care how you use them.' . . . Jashoda had forever scrubbed her breasts carefully with soap and oil, for the master's sons had put the nipples in their mouth. Why did those breasts betray her in the end? . . . Knowing

> these breasts to be the rice winner she had constantly conceived to keep them filled with milk.

Just as the wage-worker cannot distinguish between necessary and surplus labor, so the gendered 'proletarian'—serving the *oikos* rather than the *polis* with nothing but her (power to produce) offspring—comes to call the so-called sanctity of motherhood into question. At first Mahasweta broaches it derisively:

> Is a Mother so cheaply made?
> Not just by dropping a babe.

Finally it becomes a part of Jashoda's last sentient judgment:

> 'If you suckle you're a mother, all lies! Nepal and Gopal don't look at me, and the Master's boys don't spare a peek to ask how I'm doing.' The sores on her breast kept mocking her with a hundred mouths, a hundred eyes.

By contrast, her final judgment, the universalization of foster-motherhood, is a 'mistake':

> The doctor who sees her every day, the person who will cover her face with a sheet, will put her on a cart, will lower her at the burning ghat, the untouchable who will put her in the furnace, are all her milk-sons.

Such a judgment can only be 'right' within the pieties of Mahasweta's own nationalist reading.

The Marxian fable of a transition from the domestic to the 'domestic' mode of social reproduction has no more than a strained plausibility here. In order to construct it, one must entertain a grounding assumption, that the originary state of 'necessary labour' is where the lactating mother produces a use value. For whose use? If you consider her in a subject-position, it is a situation of exchange, with the child, for immediate and future psycho-social affect. Even if we read the story as a proto-nationalist parable about Mother India, it is the failure of this exchange that is the substance of the story. It is this failure, the absence of the child as such, that is marked by the enigmatic answer-question-parataxis toward the conclusion: 'Yet someone was supposed to be there at the end. Who was it? It was who? Who was it? Jashoda died at 11 p.m.'

By dismantling (professional) motherhood and suckling into their minute particulars, 'Stanadayini' allows us to differentiate ourselves from the axiomatics of a certain 'Marxist-feminism' which is obliged to ignore the subaltern woman as subject.

If Lise Vogel, from whom I drew my representative generalization, signals a certain orthodoxy, Anne Ferguson, in 'On Conceiving Motherhood,' shows us a way out of it via the question of affect:

> Although different societies have had different modes of sex/affective production at different times, a cross-cultural constant is involved in different modes of bourgeois patriarchal sex/affective production. This is that women as mothers are placed in a structural bind by mother-centered infant and small child care, a bind that ensures that mothers will give more

> than they get in the sex/affective parenting triangle in which even lesbian and single parents are subjected.[30]

'Mothers will give more than they get.' If this broad generalization is broadened so that the distinction between domestic ('natural' mother) and 'domestic' (waged wet-nurse) disappears, this can certainly serve as a constant for us and can be a good tool for our students.[31] Yet it should also be acknowledged that such a broadening might make us misrepresent important details. A text such as 'Stanadayini,' even if taught as nothing but sociological evidence, can show how imprecise it is to write: 'In stratified class and caste societies, different economic classes and racial/ethnic groups may hold different sex/gender ideals, although when this happens the lower classes are usually categorized as inferior male and female types by nature.'[32] (I am referring, of course, to the class-subalternity of the Brahmin and the grotesque functioning of caste markers within subalternity. Jashoda is a complicit victim of all these factors.) It is possible that it is not only 'the relationship between the three domination systems [class, racial/ethnic, and sex/gender]' that is 'dialectical,' but that in the theatres of decolonization, the relationship between indigenous and imperialist systems of domination are also 'dialectical,' even when they are variously related to the Big Three Systems cited above. Indeed, the relationship might not be 'dialectical' at all but discontinuous, 'interruptive.'

It is often the case that revisionist socialist-feminism trivializes basic issues in the Marxist system.[33] Ferguson writes, for example: 'My theory, unlike one tendency within classic marxist theory, does not privilege the economic realm (the production of *things* to meet human material needs and the manner in which the social surplus gets appropriated) as the material base for all human domination relations. . . . The production of things and the production of people . . . interpenetrate.'[34]

This is an excellent advance on generalizations such as Vogel's. But it is an oversimplification of Marx's view of the economic sphere. That sphere is the site of the production of *value*, not *things*. As I have mentioned earlier, it is the body's susceptibility to the production of value which makes it vulnerable to idealization and therefore to insertion into the economic. This is the ground of the labour theory of value. It is here that the story of the emergence of value from Jashoda's labour-power infiltrates Marxism and questions its gender-specific presuppositions. The production of people through sexual reproduction and affective socialization, on the other hand, presupposes mothers embodied not as female humans but only as mothers and belongs properly speaking to the sphere of politics and ideology (domination).[35] Of course it interpenetrates the economic sphere (exploitation), the sphere of the production of value, of the sustained alienation of the body to which the very nature of labour-power makes the body susceptible. In spite of the greatest sympathy for the mother, Ferguson's ignoring of the mother's body obliges her to ignore the woman as subject of the production of value. 'Stanadayini''s lesson may be simply this: when the economic as such (here shown in terms of the woman's body) enters in, mothers are divided, women can exploit, not merely dominate.

Ideology sustains and interpenetrates this operation of exploitation.

Anna Davin's meticulous 'Imperialism and Motherhood' shows us the development of sex/affective control within the context of class-struggle. ('Imperialism' and 'War' here are political signifiers used for ideological mobilization.)[36] In Davin's account, the great narrative of the development of capitalism is untroubled by discontinuities and interruptions. She describes the construction of the British National Subject of the bodies of British mothers.[37] Public opinion is under active construction so that the working of the privates may be adjudicated. *Mutatis mutandis*, echoes of these arguments from eugenics and educated mothercraft can be heard among the Indian indigenous elite today. The space where Jashoda, burdened by her ideological production, nourishes her cancer, is not accessible to that narrative.

In Davin's essay, the central reference point is class. The *oikos* is fully a metaphor for the *polis*. Foster-mothers are Virgin Mothers. Christianity, the official religion, gives a little help to the ideology of the secular state.

The lack of fit between this neat narrative and the bewildering cacophony of 'Stanadayini' permits us to ask: why globalize? Why should a sociological study that makes astute generalizations about sex/affective production in the United States feel obliged to produce a 'cross-cultural constant'? Why should a study that exposes gender-mobilization in Britain purport to speak on the relationship between imperialism and motherhood? Why, on the contrary, does 'Stanadayini' invoke the singularity of the gendered subaltern? What is at stake here? How are these stakes different from those of imperialism as such? The story will make us come back to these questions.

Elite approaches: 'Stanadayini' in Liberal Feminism

There is a tendency in the US towards homogenizing and reactive critical descriptions of Third World literatures. There is a second tendency, not necessarily related to the first, to pedagogic and curricular appropriation of Third World women's texts in translation by feminist teachers and readers who are vaguely aware of the race-bias within mainstream feminism: 'Black and Third World feminist organizations are thus developing within different racial and ethnic communities as an attempt to resolve intra-community the social crisis of the family and personal intimacy presently occurring across racial/ethnic lines. Influential members and groups within the white women's movements are presently seeking to make coalitions with black feminists, in part by dealing with the racism within the white women's movement.'[38]

There are problems with this basically benevolent impulse which are increasingly under scrutiny.[39] The ravenous hunger for Third World literary texts in English translation is part of the benevolence and the problem. Since by translating this text I am contributing to both, I feel obliged to notice the text's own relationship to the thematics of liberal feminism. This will permit me also to touch directly the question of elite approaches to subaltern material.

Resisting 'elite' methodology for 'subaltern' material involves an epistemological/ontological confusion. The confusion is held in an unacknowledged analogy: just as the subaltern *is* not elite (ontology), so must the historian not *know* through elite method (epistemology).

This is part of a much larger confusion: can men theorize feminism, can whites theorize racism, can the bourgeois theorize revolution and so on.[40] It is when only the former groups theorize that the situation is politically intolerable. Therefore it is crucial that members of these groups are kept vigilant about their assigned subject-positions. It is disingenuous, however, to forget that, as the collectivities implied by the second group of nouns start participating in the production of knowledge about themselves, they must have a share in some of the structures of privileges that contaminate the first group. (Otherwise the ontological errors are perpetuated: it is unfortunate simply to *be* a woman—now a man; to *be* a black—now a white; and to be subaltern—now elite—is only the fault of the individual.) Therefore did Gramsci speak of the subaltern's rise into hegemony; and Marx of associated labour benefitting from 'the forms that are common to all social modes of production.'[41] This is also the reason behind one of the assumptions of subalternist work: that the subaltern's own idiom did not allow him to *know* his struggle so that he could articulate himself as its subject. If the woman/black/subaltern, possessed through struggle of some of the structures previously metonymic as man/white/elite, continues to exercise a self-marginalized purism, and if the benevolent members of the man/white/elite participate in the marginalization and thus legitimate the bad old days, we have a caricature of correct politics that leaves alone the field of continuing subalternization. It is the *loneliness* of the gendered subaltern that is staged in 'Stanadayini.'

(The position that only the subaltern can know the subaltern, only women can know women and so on, cannot be held as a theoretical presupposition either, for it predicates the possibility of knowledge on identity. Whatever the political necessity for holding the position, and whatever the advisability of attempting to 'identify' (with) the other as subject in order to know her, knowledge is made possible and is sustained by irreducible difference, not identity. What is known is always in excess of knowledge. Knowledge is never adequate to its object. The theoretical model of the ideal knower in the embattled position we are discussing is that of the person identical with her predicament. This is actually the figure of the impossibility and non-necessity of knowledge. Here the relationship between the practical—need for claiming subaltern identity—and the theoretical—no program of knowledge production can presuppose identity as origin —is, once again, of an 'interruption' that persistently brings each term to crisis.)

By drawing attention to the complicity between hegemonic (here US) and orthodox (here Indian) readings, I have been attempting to attend to the continuing subalternization of Third World material. At this point, I hope it will come as no surprise that a certain version of the elite vs. subaltern position is perpetuated by non-Marxist anti-racist feminism in the Anglo-US toward Third World women's texts in translation. (The group covers the spectrum from anti-Marxism through romantic anti-capitalism into corporatism—I will call the ensemble 'liberal feminism' for terminological convenience.) The position is exacerbated by the fact that liberal feminist Third Worldist criticism often chooses as its constituency the indigenous post-colonial elite, diasporic or otherwise.

If Mahasweta's text displaces the Marxist-feminist terms of the analysis of domestic labour, it also calls into question this liberal-feminist choice. It dramatizes indigenous class-formation under imperialism and its connection to the movement towards women's social emancipation. In the strong satiric voice of authorial comment she writes of the patriarch Haldar: 'He made his cash in the British era, when *Divide and Rule* was the policy. Haldarbabu's mentality was constructed then . . . During the Second War . . . he helped the anti-Fascist struggle of the Allies by buying and selling scrap iron.' The mind set of the imperialist is displaced and replicated in the comprador capitalist. If 'East and West' meant a global division for the imperialist, within the minute heterogeneous cartography of this post-colonial space, the phrase comes to indicate East and West Bengal. East Bengal (today's Bangladesh) has a phantasmatic status as a proper name, an indigenous division now merely alluding to the imperial and pre-imperial past. Haldar identifies in no way with the parts of 'India' outside of this 'Bengal': 'he doesn't trust anyone—not a Punjabi-Oriya-Bihari-Gujarati-Marathi-Muslim'.

This sentence is an echo of a well-known line from the Indian national anthem, an obvious cultural monument: 'Punjaba-Sindhu-Gujarata-Maratha-Dravida-Utkala (Orissa)-Banġa (Bengal).' A national anthem is a regulative metonym for the identity of a nation. Mahasweta's mocking enumeration, describing the country metonymically even as it alludes to that regulative metonym, the anthem, measures the distance between regulation and constitution. This measure then reflects back upon the declarative sentence about secular India that opens the passage we are reading: 'He lives in independent India, the India that makes no distinctions among people, kingdoms, languages . . .' The reader cannot find a stable referent for the ill-treated Mother India of Mahasweta's reading.

Even in the archaic 'East Bengal' that seems to be the space of Haldar's 'national' identity (Mahasweta's word is 'patriotism'), Dhaka, Mymensingh, Jashore—the celebrated cities, towns, areas are found wanting. 'Harisal,' the man's birthplace, is claimed as the fountainhead of that most hegemonic construct, the cultural heritage of ancient India: 'One day it will emerge that the *Vedas* and the *Upanishads* were also written in Harisal'. Of course a lot of this relies for effect on the peculiar humour of the two Bengals. But surely to tie, as 'Stanadayini' does, this kind of molecular chauvinism to the divisive operations of imperialism is to warn against its too-quick definition as Hegel's 'childhood of history,' transferred to Adorno's caution in *Minima Moralia* against 'pre-capitalist peoples,' percolated into Habermas's careless admission that his defence of the ethico-politics of modernism had to be, alas, Eurocentric, or into Kristeva's impassioned call to protect the future of the European illusion against the incursions of a savage Third World[42]

This appropriation of a 'national' identity is not the 'taking on [of] an essentialist temptation for internationalist purposes.'[43] Internationalist stakes are a remote presence here. This 'national' self-situation is marked by a contradiction, a failure of the desire for essence. First it seeks to usurp the origins of Brahminism, the *Vedas* and the *Upanishads.* Next it declares itself dissolved by a Brahmin: 'There's no East or West for a Brahmin. If there's a sacred thread around his neck [the sign of being a Brahmin] you have to give him respect even when he's taking a shit.' This two-step standing in for identity, is a cover for the brutalizing of the Brahmin when the elite in caste is subaltern in class. (In the case of class-manipulation, 'poverty [is] the fault of the individuals, not an intrinsic part of a class society'; in the case of caste-manipulation, the implicit assumption is the reverse: the Brahmin is systemically excellent, not necessarily so as an individual.)[44]

I have gone through the rich texture of the description of Haldar as 'patriot' (nationalism reduced to absurdity) because, although he is a patriarch, it is through their access to the circuit of his political, economic, and ideological production ('he had made his cash in the British era . . . [his] mentality was constructed then') that the Haldar women move into a species of reproductive emancipation seemingly outside of patriarchal control. Jashoda the 'proletarian' is only useful at the first stage:

> Jashoda's worth went up in the Haldar house. The husbands are pleased because the wives' knees no longer knock when they riffle the almanac. Since their children are being reared on Jashoda's milk, they can be the Holy Child in bed at will. The wives no longer have an excuse to say 'no.' The wives are happy. They can keep their figures. They can wear blouses and bras of 'European cut.' After

keeping the fast of Shiva's night by watching all-night picture shows they are no longer obliged to breast-feed their babies.

But the transition from domestic to 'domestic' has no place in the greater narrative where women's ideological liberation has its class fix: 'In the matter of motherhood, the old lady's granddaughters-in-law had breathed a completely different air before they crossed her threshold . . . The old man had dreamed of filling half Calcutta with Haldars. The granddaughters-in-law were unwilling. Defying the old lady's tongue, they took off to their husbands' places of work.'

Another step and we are free to fantasize an entry in to the world of many of Bharati Mukherjee's earlier heroines, Indian wives whose husbands' places of work are in the United States.[45] If they start going to school on the side, we have the privileged native informants of liberal third worldist feminism. Can we not imagine Haldar *daughters* of this generation going off to graduate school on their own, rebels and heroines suckled on Jashoda's milk, full-fledged feminists, writing pieces such as 'The Betrayal of Superwoman':

> We must learn to be vocal in expressing, without guilt or embarrassment, what our careers mean to us. It is not something on the side that we can abandon at will to take up career moves of a husband that we were not included in discussing . . . We must reach out to other women who think they are alone, share our experiences and be each other's support. We need to accept ourselves as Women Who Never Learned To Do Macramé and Do Not Plan Their Weekend Social Life until

> Friday Afternoon. We are sad. But we are glad. This is what we will always be.[46]

There is a complete absence of history or of subject position in this passage written by a woman of the Indian diaspora in the United States. Mahasweta's Jashoda dies in the 1980s, of the history that allows this diasporic woman to say 'this is what we will *always* be.' The critical deployment of liberal feminist thematics in Mahasweta's text obliges us to remember that 'we' in this passage might be parasitical not only upon imperialism (Haldar) but upon the gendered subaltern (Jashoda) as well. Fiction and its pedagogy can here perform the ideological mobilization of a moral economy that a mere benevolent tracing of the historical antecedents of the speaker might not be able to. The two must go together as each other's 'interruption,' for the burden of proof lies upon historical research. It is to belabour the obvious to say that structures of logical and legal-model scholarly demonstrations alone cannot bring about counter-hegemonic ideological production.

It might be worth mentioning here that the left fringe of liberal feminism would like to correct Marxism by defining woman as a sexual class.[47] Again, it is possible to appreciate the situational force of this as an attempt to ensure that women's problems are not demeaned. But if this so-called correction is entertained theoretically, then the call to unity might carry the imprint of the academic or corporatist class among women.

In this context, Mahasweta's own reading can be extended into plausibility. The granddaughters-in-law leave the household (a relic of imperialism) and thus deprive Jashoda of her means of livelihood, however grotesque. This can be decoded as the post-Independence Indian diaspora, specifically as part of the 'brain drain.' It is a tribute to the story that no direct 'logical' or 'scientific' connection exists between this departure and Jashoda's disease and death, just as none can be established between the nature of Jashoda's labour and her end. Strictly speaking, *whatever the pathology of her disease,* what would have saved her is better medical care. I have tried to show so far that the prehistory and peculiar nature of her disease, since they involve unequal gendering, are crucial if 'Stanadayini' is to become a text for use.

Jashoda's story is thus not that of the development of a feminine subjectivity, a female *Bildungsroman,* which is the ideal of liberal feminist literary criticism. This is not to say that Jashoda is a 'static' character. To go back to my opening remarks, the development of character or the understanding of subjectivity as growth in consciousness is beside the point of this parable or of this representation of the subaltern. That road not taken is marked by the progress of the granddaughters-in-law. To place the subaltern in a subject-position in her history is not necessarily to make her an individualist.

Inhabiting the shifting line between parable and representation, undoing the opposition between tenor and vehicle, Mahasweta's Jashoda also expands the thematics of the woman's political body. Within liberal feminism, the feminist body politic is defined by the struggle for reproductive rights.

It is of course of central importance to establish women's right to practise or withhold reproduction. A text such as 'Stanadayini,' by posing the double scene of Jashoda as both subaltern (representation rather than character) and parabolic sign, reminds us that the crucial struggle must be situated within a much larger network where feminism is obliged to lose the clear race- and class-specific contours which depend upon an *exclusive* identification of woman with reproductive or copulating body. (Black and Hispanic working-class women in the US have already made this point with reference to the ignoring of enforced sterilization in favour of the right to abortion; but this is still to remain within the identification of woman with the body defined minimally.) When the woman's body is used only as a metaphor for a nation (or anything else) feminists correctly object to the effacement of the materiality of that body. Mahasweta's own reading, taken too literally, might thus transgress the power of her text. But, in that shadow area where Jashoda is a signifier for subalternity as such, as well as a metaphor for the predicament of the decolonized nation-state 'India', we are forced, once again, to distance ourselves from the identity of Woman with the female copulative and reproductive body.

In the story, having children is also accession to free labour, the production of surplus that can be appropriated with no apparent extra-economic coercion. (Almost incidentally, 'Stanadayini' undoes the line between consenting and coercive sexual intercourse (rape) without the facile reference to free libidinal choice.[48]) As such the solution to Jashoda's problem cannot be mere reproductive rights but productive rights as well. And these rights are denied her not just by men, but by elite women as well. This is the underlying paradox of population control in the Third World.[49] To oppose reproductive rights with the casuistical masculist pseudo-concern about the 'right to life' cannot be relevant here or elsewhere.[50] Yet to oppose productive rights with the so-called 'right to work' laws cannot be the only issue either, precisely because the subject here is female, and the question is not only of class but of gender.

Again, 'Stanadayini' can offer no precise answers, no documented evidence. Taught as a text for use, it can raise constructive questions, corrective doubts.

'Elite' Approaches: 'Stanadayini' in a Theory of Woman's Body

Used as a teachable text, 'Stanadayini' calls into question that aspect of Western Marxist feminism which, from the point of view of work, trivializes the theory of value and, from the point of view of mothering as work, ignores the mother as subject. It calls into question that aspect of Western Liberal Feminism which privileges the indigenous or diasporic elite from the Third World and identifies Woman with the reproductive or copulative body. So-called Feminist 'Theory,' generally associated with developments in France of the last thirty years, is perceived as unrealistic and elitist by the two former groups.[51] I do not wish to enter that sterile quarrel. I submit that if 'Stanadayini' is made to intervene in some thematics of this esoteric theoretical era, it can show up some of the limits of that space as well.

I will keep myself restricted to the question of *jouissance* as orgasmic pleasure. If to identify woman with her copulative or reproductive body can be seen as minimalizing and reductive, woman's orgasmic pleasure, taking place in excess of copulation or reproduction, can be seen as a way out of such reductive identifications. There is a great deal of rather diverse writing on the subject.[52] Mahasweta's text seems to be silent on the issue. I have heard a Bengali woman writer remark in public, 'Mahasweta Devi writes like a man.' I will therefore consider a man's text about women's silence: 'A Love Letter,' by Jacques Lacan.[53]

In this essay Lacan gives a rather terse formulation of a point of view that he developed throughout his career: 'The unconscious presupposes that *in* the speaking being there is something, somewhere, which knows more than he does.'[54] If this is taken to mean that the subject (speaking being) is more like a map or graph of knowing rather than an individual self that knows, a limit to the claim to power of knowledge is inscribed. The formulation belongs with such experiments as those epistemographs (maps of stages of knowing rather than the story of the growth of an individual mind that knows) of Hegel that the early Lukacs used so brilliantly as charts of 'immanent meaning'; the Marxian notion of ideology; and the Barthesian notion of the writable text that is not readable as such.[55] Fredric Jameson has recently expanded this specifically Lacanian position into the 'political unconscious.'[56]

If we take Lacan at his word here, this knowing-place, writing itself and writing us, 'others' the self. It is a map of the speaking being that is beyond its own grasp as other. Thought is where this knowing-program, the mapping of knowledge, exceeds itself into and thus outlines the deliberative consciousness. Since this epistemograph is also what constitutes the subject (as well as 'others' it), knowing in this para-subjective sense is also being. (If we understand this being-that-is-a-map-of-the-known as the socio-political and historical ensemble, collectively constituting the subject not fully knowable, this would produce materiality preceding or containing consciousness.)[57] It is in this sense that Lacan writes: 'As against the being upheld by philosophical tradition, that is the being residing in thought and taken to be its correlate, I argue that we are played by *jouissance*. Thought is *jouissance* . . . There is a *jouissance* of being.[58]

Thought, as *jouissance*, is not orgasmic pleasure genitally defined, but the excess of being that escapes the circle of the reproduction of the subject. It is the mark of the Other in the subject. Now psychoanalysis can only ever conceive of thought as possible through those mechanics of signification where the phallus comes to *mean* the Law by positing castration as punishment as such. Although the point is made repeatedly by Lacan that we are not speaking of the actual male member but of the phallus as the signifier, it is still obviously a gendered position. Thus when thought thinks itself a place that cannot be known, that always escapes the proof of reproduction, it thinks according to Lacan, of the *jouissance* of the woman.[59]

If one attempted to figure this out without presupposing the identity of the male-gendered position and the position of the thinking (speaking) subject, the singularity and asymmetry of woman's *jouissance* would still seem undeniable in a heterosexually organized world. It would still escape the closed circle of the theoretical fiction of pleasured reproduction-in-copulation as use-value.[60] It would still be the place where an unexchangeable excess can be imagined and figured forth. *This*, rather than male-gendered thought, is woman's *jouissance* in the general sense.

I cannot agree with Lacan that woman's *jouissance* in the narrow sense, 'the opposition between [so-called] vaginal satisfaction and clitoral orgasm ' is 'fairly trivial.'[61] We cannot compute the line where *jouissance* in the general sense shifts into *jouissance* in the narrow sense. But we can propose that, because *jouissance* is where an unexchangeable excess is tamed into exchange, where 'what is this' slides into 'what is this worth' slides into 'what does this mean?' *it* (rather than castration) is where signification emerges. Women's liberation, women's access to autobiography, women's access to the ambivalent arena of thought, must remain implicated in this taming. Thus, to call Mahasweta's preoccupation in 'Stanadayini' with *jouissance* in the general sense 'writing like a man' is to reduce a complex position to the trivializing simplicity of a hegemonic gendering.

Jouissance in general: Jashoda's body

In 'Stanadayini' Jashoda's body, rather than her fetishized deliberative consciousness (self or subjectivity), is the *place* of knowledge, rather than the instrument of knowing. This cannot be an argument. Literary language, as it is historically defined, allows us no more than to take a persistent distance from the rationalist project, shared by the social sciences, radical or otherwise. This distancing is a supplement to the project. It could never have the positive role of an opposition. The role of Jashoda's body as the place where the sinister knowledge of decolonization as failure of foster-mothering is figured forth produces cancer, an excess very far from the singularity of the clitoral orgasm.

The speech of the Other is recorded in a cryptic sentence. It is a response to Jashoda's last 'conscious' or 'rational' judgement: '"If you suckle you're a mother, all lies" . . . The sores on her breast kept mocking her with a hundred mouths, a hundred eyes.'

This is the only time the Other 'speaks.' The disease has not been diagnosed or named yet. The Other inhabits a hundred eyes and mouths, a transformation of the body's inscription into a disembodied yet anthropomorphic agency, which makes of the breast, the definitive female organ within the circle of reproduction, (a) pluralized almost-face.[62] (The metonymic construction common in Bengali colloquial usage should literally be translated 'in a hundred mouths' et cetera, 'meaning,' of course, also *with.*) Does the Other agree or disagree with Jashoda's judgement about the identity of the mother, so crucial to the story? 'Mocking' tells us nothing.

Consider for a moment the phrase that I have translated, 'kept mocking': *Byango korte thaklo.*

The first noticeable thing here is the lack of synchronization between Jashoda's judgement and the response. The latter is sustained—'*kept* mocking'—as if Jashoda's remarks were merely an interruption. (We recall that the remarks had been made in the mistaken assumption that her husband was still in the room. Even as normal intersubjective exchange, it is a failure.) One may put discourse into the mouth and eyes of a displaced and disembodied Other. One cannot fabricate an intersubjective dialogue with it. The status of the cancer as the figuring of the *jouissance* of the subaltern female body as thought-in-decolonization is thus kept intact here.

Let us focus on the word *byango*—translatable loosely as 'mock[ery]'. the word *ango*—body (with organs) as opposed to *deho*—the body as a whole—makes itself felt within it. The Sanskrit source word *vyangya* meant, primarily, deformed. The secondary meaning—mockery—indicated the specific mockery that is produced by a contortion of the body, by deforming one's form. Modern Bengali has lost the sense that, in Sanskrit, would consolidate the reading that I am trying to produce: the implicit meaning that can only be understood through (gestural) suggestion.[63] When language de-forms itself and gestures at you, mocking signification, there is *byango*. The limit of meaning, the *jouissance* of the female body politic, is marked in this sentence.

This is altogether different from using the cancer simply as another metaphor invading the metaphor of the sexually undifferentiated body politic, listed in Susan Sontag's *Illness as Metaphor*.[64] It is interesting to see how different the history of cancer as metaphor is in the context of the last couple of centuries in the Anglo-US. The emphasis there is basically psychologistic: 'the disease is what speaks through the body, language for dramatizing the *mental*.'[65] From within this history, Sontag calls for a 'de-metaphorization' of the disease.

This brings up two widely separated issues: philosophically, can anything be absolutely de-metaphorized? and politically, is it necessary in order to bring the theatre of decolonization into such a de-metaphorized arena of reality, to drag it through the various stages of comprador capitalism, until it can graduate into 'expressive individualism' so that it can begin to qualify for demetaphorization? In other words, the political aspect of this suggestion must confront us with the argument for 'development.' There can be no doubt that situational agents of 'development,' especially counter-diasporic indigenous service professionals like 'Stanadayini''s doctor, are often selfless and good. Yet it must be noticed that, if we were to read him characterologically, he would be the only character who had so internalized bureaucratic egalitarianism as to judge Jashoda by an absolute standard: 'The doctor understood that he was unreasonably angry because Jashoda was in this condition. He was angry with Jashoda, with Kangali, with women who don't take the signs of breast cancer *seriously* enough and finally die in this dreadful and hellish pain.'

Engaging the thematics of the *jouissance* of the female body, 'Stanadayini' can be read not only to show (a race-and-class-specific) gendering at work in Lacanian theory. It can also make visible the limits of a merely structural psychoanalytic strategy of reading.

In 'A Love Letter,' Lacan rewrites 'I think, therefore I am' in the following way: 'There is . . . an animal which finds himself speaking [taken to presume or entail 'thinking'], and for whom it follows that, by inhabiting [occupying with desire and mastery, *besetzend,* cathecting] the signifier, he is its subject.'[66] If one is sympathetic to the critique of the sovereign subject, one does not have trouble accepting this as a persistent caution. 'From then on, everything is played out for him on the level of fantasy, but a fantasy which can perfectly well be taken apart so as to allow for the fact that he knows a great deal more than he thinks when he acts.'

Knowledge is played out or mapped out on the entire map of the speaking being, thought is the *jouissance* or excess of being. We have already drawn out the implications of this position in our discussion of Jashoda's body as the *place* of knowing in the text. But, in order 'to take apart' the fantasy inhabiting this text 'perfectly' one would have to part company with the psychoanalytic scenario.

I have speculated elsewhere that a narrative of sanctioned suicide (rather than castration) might begin to limn a 'Hindu' phantasmatic order.[67] Rather than the stories of Oedipus (signification) and Adam (salvation), the multiple narratives of situated suicide might then regulate a specifically 'Hindu' sense of the progress of life. (These narratives are 'regulative psychobiographies.') When we begin to consider the question of a 'perfect' analysis, we have to analyse the subalternization of indigenous psychobiographic narratives. The institutionalization of psychoanalysis, the establishment of its claim to scientificity (within which one must situate Lacan's critique), and its imposition upon the colonies, has its own history.[68] A question similar to some I have already posed emerges here also: should the access to hegemony of an indigenous (here 'Hindu') regulative psychobiography lie through the necessary access to an institutionalization, like that of psychoanalysis, entailing the narrative of imperialist political economy? Within feminist 'theory,' we are caught in only the *gendering* rather than the overtly imperialist politics of psychoanalysis.

Given such matters, it might be interesting to measure the distance between Lacan's connecting of woman's *jouissance* and the naming of God on the one hand, and the end of 'Stanadayini' on the other. Lacan moves the question, 'can the woman say anything about *jouissance*?' asked by a man, to the point where the woman also confronts the question of the Other:

> for in this she is herself subjected to the Other just as much as the man. Does the Other know? . . . If god does not know hatred, it is clear for Empedocles that he knows less than mortals . . . which might lead one to say that the more man may ascribe to the woman in confusion with God, that is, in confusion with what it is she comes from, the less he hates, the lesser he is, and since after all, there is no love without hate, the less he loves.[69]

At the end of Mahasweta's story Jashoda herself is said to 'be God manifest.' This is inconsistent with the logic of the rest of the narrative, where Jashoda is clearly being played by the exigencies of the Haldar household. It is also a sudden and serious introduction of the discourse of philosophical monotheism in what has so far been a satiric indexing of the ideological use of goddesses (*Singhabahini* or the Lionseated) and mythic god-women (the 'original' Jashoda of Hindu mythology). Here at the conclusion the gender of the agent is unspecified. (The English translation obliges us to choose a gender.) Is it possible that, because Mahasweta Devi does not present this conclusion from a male-gendered position, we are not reduced to man's affective diminution when he puts woman in the place of God? Is it possible that we have here, not the discourse of castration but of sanctioned suicide? 'Jashoda was God manifest, others do and did whatever she thought. Jashoda's death was also the death of God'. Does Jashoda's death spell out a species of *icchamrityu*—willed death—the most benign form of sanctioned suicide within Hindu regulative psychobiography? Can a woman have access to *icchamrityu*—a category of suicide arising out of *tatvajnana* or the knowledge of the 'it'-ness of the subject? The question of gendering here is not psychoanalytic or counterpsychoanalytic. It is the question of woman's access to that paradox of the knowledge of the limits of knowledge where the strongest assertion of agency, to negate the possibility of agency, cannot be an example of itself as suicide.[70] 'Stanadayini' affirms this access through the (dis)figuring of the Other in the (woman's) body rather than the possibility of transcendence in the (man's) mind. Read in the context of *icchamrityu*, the last sentence of the text becomes deeply ambivalent. Indeed, the positive or negative value of the statement becomes undecidable: 'When a mortal plays God here below, she is forsaken by all and she must always die alone.'

Over against what might be seen as the 'serious' laying out of the thematics of woman's *jouissance* in the general sense, there is rather a strange moment that might be read as indicating the inscrutability of woman's *jouissance* in the narrow sense.

'Stanadayini' opens with a general description of Jashoda as a professional mother. Immediately following, there is a brief narrative sequence, embedded in other, even briefer, references, the logical irrelevance of which the text is at pains to point out: 'But these matters are mere blind alleys. Motherhood did not become Jashoda's profession for these afternoon-whims.'

The sequence deals with the cook. Like Jashoda, she loses her job as a result of the youngest Haldar-son's clandestine activities: 'He stole his mother's ring, slipped it into the cook's pillowcase, raised a hue and cry, and got the cook kicked out'. We do not know the end of her story. In terms of narrative value, the cook is the real marginal. It is in her voice that the inscrutability of woman's pleasure announces itself: 'One afternoon the boy, driven by lust, attacked the cook and the cook, since her body was heavy with rice, stolen fishheads and turnip greens and her body languid with sloth, lay back, saying, "Yah, do what you like." [Afterwards] . . . he wept repentant tears, mumbling "Auntie, don't tell." The cook—saying, "What's there to tell?"—went quickly to sleep.'

(I am not suggesting that we should give in to our body's depradations and refuse to testify—just as, at the other end of the scale of cultural control—no one would suggest that the text about sex-affective production called *King Lear* invites people to go mad and walk about in storms. If what we are combating as teachers is liberal-nationalist-universalist humanism with its spurious demands for the autonomy of art and the authority of the author, we must be ready to admit that the demand that plots be directly imitable in politically corrrect action leads to the extravagances of 'socialist' or 'feminist' realism and a new Popular Front.)

In the voice of the marginal who disappears from the story, in between the uncaring 'do what you like' and 'what's there to tell,' Mahasweta might be marking the irreducible inscrutability of the pleasure of the woman's body.[71] This is not the rhapsodic high artistic language of elite feminist literary experimentation. Escaping the reducible logic (including the authorial reading *and* the pedagogic interventions) of the story, this exchange is clothed in slang. As Gautam Bhadra has pointed out, it is in the unfreezable dynamic of slang that subaltern semiosis hangs out.[72]

What, indeed, is there to tell? The cook, a non-character in the story, could not have *intended* the rhetorical question *seriously*. It is almost as if what is told, the story of Jashoda, is the result of an obstinate misunderstanding of the rhetorical question that transforms the condition of the (im)-possibility of answering—of telling the story—into the condition of its possibility.[73] Every production of experience, thought, knowledge, all humanistic disciplinary production, perhaps especially the representation of the subaltern in history or literature, has this double bind at its origin.

The influential French feminist theorist Julia Kristeva has proposed a rewriting of the Freudian version of the Oedipal family romance. She theorizes an 'abject' mother who, unequally coupled with the 'imaginary' father, offers a primary narcissistic model which allows the infant to speak.[74] The focus here is unwaveringly on the child—and, since Kristeva is an apologist for Christianity—upon the Holy Child. If some details of the iconography of the abject mother seem to fit Jashoda's predicament, we should, I think, resist the seduction of a lexicon that beckons to a coherent reading by strategically excluding the entire political burden of the text. There can be no similarity between Kristeva's positing of a pre-originary space where sexual difference is annulled—so that a benignly Christian *agape* can be seen to pre-date *Eros* on the one hand, and the sinister vision of the failure of social cement in a decolonized space where questions of genital pleasure or social affect are framed, on the other.[75]

One cannot of course compare analytical discussions of ideology with psychoanalytical reconstructions of interpellation.[76] Kristeva's discussions of the place of the Virgin within cultural Subject-representation and constitution are, however, so close to isomorphic generalizations that I think they might be productively contrasted to Mahasweta's critique of the nationwide patriarchal mobilization of the Hindu Divine Mother and Holy Child. Her treatment of an active polytheism focuses the possibility that there are many accesses to the mother-child scene. The story plays itself out between two cultural uses of it. The figure of the all-willing Lionseated, whose official icon of motherhood triumphant is framed by her many adult divine children, democratically dividing the governance of the many sectors of the manifest world, is reflected in the temple quarter of Calcutta. The figure of the all-nurturing Jashoda provides the active principle of patriarchal sexual ideology. As in the case of her earlier short story 'Draupadi,' Mahasweta mobilizes the figure of the mythic female as opposed to the full-fledged goddess. Kristeva points at the Virgin's asymmetrical status as the Mother of God by constructing the imaginary father and the abject mother.[77] Mahasweta introduces exploitation/domination into that detail in the mythic story which tells us that Jashoda is a *foster*-mother. By turning fostering into a profession, she sees mothering in its materiality beyond its socialization as affect, beyond psychologization as abjection, or yet transcendentalization as the vehicle of the divine.

Considerations Specifically of Gendering

A few more remarks on the economy of the Lionseated and Jashoda are in order here.

A basic technique of representing the subaltern as such (of either sex) is as the object of the gaze 'from above.'[78] It is noticeable that whenever Jashoda is represented in this way in 'Stanadayini,' the eye-object situation is deflected into a specifically religious discourse. In Hindu polytheism the god or goddess, as indeed, *mutatis mutandis* the revered person, is also an object of the gaze, 'from below.' Through a programmed confounding of the two kinds of gaze goddesses can be used to dissimulate women's oppression.[79] The transformation of the final cause of the entire chain of events in the first part of the narrative into the will of the Lionseated is an example of how the latter is used to dissimulate Jashoda's exploitation. For the sufficient cause is, as we well know, the cheating and spoiled youngest Haldar son with the genital itch. In the following passage, it is he who is the subject of the gaze, the object being the suckling Jashoda, a sort of living icon of the mythic Jashoda the Divine (Foster) Mother suckling the Holy Child. The man (the one above) thus masquerades as the one below, so that the subaltern can be dissimulated into an icon. Displaced into that iconic role, she can then be used to declare the will of the dominant Female, the goddess Lionseated: 'One day as the youngest son was squatting to watch Jashoda's milking, she said, '"There dear, my Lucky. All this because you swiped him in the leg. Whose wish was it then?" "The Lionseated's," said Haldar junior.'

Mahasweta presents Jashoda as constituted by patriarchal ideology. In fact, her outspoken self-confidence in the earlier part of the story comes from her ideological conviction.[80] If the text questions the distinction between rape and consenting intercourse, Jashoda the subaltern does not participate in this questioning. 'You are husband,' she will say, 'You are guru. If I forget and say no, correct me. Where after all is the pain? . . . Does it hurt a tree to bear fruit?' (She is given the same metaphor of the 'naturalness' of woman's reproductive function—one ideological cornerstone of gendering—when she reproaches the granddaughters-in-law for 'causing' the Old Mistress's death through their refusal to bear children.) She also accepts the traditional sexual division of labour: 'The man brings, the woman cooks and serves. My lot is inside out . . . Living off a wife's carcass, you call that a man?'

Indeed, Mahasweta used Jashoda the subaltern as a measure of the dominant sexual ideology of 'India.' (Here gender uniformity is more encompassing than class difference.) Over against this is a list of 'Western stereotypes, where a certain Western feminism ('Simone de Beauvoir' serves Mahasweta as a metonym) is also situated:

> Jashoda is fully an Indian woman, whose unreasonable, unreasoning, and unintelligent devotion to her husband and love for her children, whose unnatural renunciation and forgiveness have been kept alive in the popular consciousness by all Indian women . . . Her mother-love wells up as much for Kangali as for the children . . . Such is the power of the Indian soil that all women turn into mothers here and all men remain immersed in the spirit of holy childhood. Each man the Holy Child and each woman the Divine Mother. Even those who wish to deny this and wish to slap *current posters* to the effect of the 'eternal she'— Mona Lisa'—'La passionaria'—'Simone de Beauvoir —et cetera over the old ones and look at women that way are, after all, Indian cubs. It is notable that the educated Babus desire all this from women outside the home. When they cross the threshold they want the Divine Mother in the words and conduct of the revolutionary ladies.

Here the authority of the author-function is elaborately claimed. We are reminded that the story is no more than the author's construction. The allusion to another school of Bengali fiction places the story in literary history rather than the stream of reality. In an ostentatious gesture, the author recovers herself and resumes her story: 'However, it's incorrect to cultivate the habit of repeated incursions into *by-lanes* as we tell Jashoda's life story.' That Jashoda's name is also an interpellation into patriarchal ideology is thus given overt authorial sanction through the conduct of the narrative. In terms of that ideology, the fruit of Jashoda's fostering is the Krishna whose flute-playing phallocentric eroticism, and charioteering logocentric sublation of militarism into a model of correct karma, will be embraced in nineteenth - and twentieth-century Bengali nationalism as images of the private and the public.[81]

The end of the story undoes this careful distancing of the author from the gender-ideological interpellation of the protagonist. Even when Mahasweta Devi predicates her at the end by way of the defilement of institutional English on the name-tag for unclaimed corpses in the morgue ('Jashoda Devi, Hindu female'), a certain narrative irony, strengthening the author-function, seems still intact.[82] It is the three propositions at the very end that call into question the strategically well-advertised ironic stance of the author-function.

The language and terminology of these conclusive propositions remind us of those high Hindu scriptures where a merely narrative religion shifts, through the register of theology, into a species of speculative philosophy: 'Jashoda was God manifest, others do and did whatever she thought. Jashoda's death was also the death of God. When a mortal plays God here below, she is forsaken by all and she must always die alone.'

It is a common argument that the subaltern as historical subject persistently translates the discourse of religion into the discourse of militancy. In the case of the subaltern as gendered subject, 'Stanadayini' recounts the failure of such a translation. It undoes the hierarchical opposition between the Hinduism of philosophical monotheism (largely bred in its contemporary outlines by way of the culture of imperialism) and that of popular polytheism. It suggests that the arrogance of the former may be complicitous with the ideological victimage of the latter. This is managed through making indeterminate the distinction between the author-function and the protagonist's predicament. If, therefore, the story (*énoncé*) tells us of the failure of a translation or discursive displacement from religion to militancy, the text as statement (*énonciation*) participates in such a translation (now indistinguishable from its 'failure') from the discourse of religion into that of political critique.

'Stanadayini' as statement performs this by compromising the author's 'truth' as distinct from the protagonist's 'ideology.' Reading the solemn assenting judgment of the end, we can no longer remain sure if the 'truth' that has so far 'framed' the ideology has any resources without it or outside it. Just as in the case of the cook's tale, we begin to notice that the narrative has, in fact, other frames that lie outside a strictly authorial irony. One of these frames, we remember, renders the world's foster mother motherless within the text. The text's epigraph comes from the anonymous world of doggerel and the first word invokes *mashi pishi* —aunts—not mothers, not even aunts by marriage, but aunts suspended before kinship inscription, the sisters of the two unnamed parents, suspended also on the edge of nature and culture, in *Bangan*, a place whose name celebrates both forest and village.[83] If the narrative recounts the failure of affect, a counter-narrative (yet another non-story) of these curious, affectless, presumably fostering aunts threatens the coherence of our interpretation in yet another way.

It is the powerful title which holds together the

reading that we have been developing in these pages. It is not 'Stanyadayini,' the word we expect, meaning 'the suckler' or 'wet-nurse.' It is, rather, 'Stanadayini,'—the giver of the breast, of the alienated means of production, the part-object, the distinguishing organ of the female as mother. The violence of this neologism allows the cancer to become the signifier of the oppression of the gendered subaltern. It is the parasite feeding on the breast in the name of affect, consuming the body politic, 'flourishing at the expense of the human host'. The sentence is in English in the Bengali text, which allows for the word 'human.' The representative or defining human case, given in English and the objective language of science, is here female.

'Much third world fiction is still caught in realism' (whereas the international literatures of the First World have graduated into language games) is a predictable generalization. This is often the result of a lack of acquaintance with the language of the original. Mahasweta's prose is an extraordinary melange of street slang, the dialect of East Bengal, the everyday household language of family and servant, and the occasional gravity of elegant Bengali. The deliberately awkward syntax conveys by this mixture an effect far from 'realistic,' although the individual elements are representationally accurate to the last degree. (I have not been able to reproduce this in the translation.) In addition, the structural conduct of the story has a fabulistic cast: the telescoped and improbable list of widespread changes in the household and locality brought about by the transition from domestic to 'domestic,' and the quick narrative of the thirty years of decolonization with its exorbitant figures, are but two examples.

What is most interesting for my purposes, however, is that the text's own comment on realism in literature should be given in terms of gendering. Just as a naive understanding of a realistic style is that it is true to life, so is it a politically naive and pernicious understanding of gendering that it is true to nature. Mahasweta's rendering of the truth of gendering in realism is so deliberately mysterious and absurd that it is almost incomprehensible even to the native speaker. The reference is to Saratchandra Chatterjee, the greatest sentimental realist in Bengali literature. No ethnographic or sociological explication of the 'connotation' of 'wood apple nectar' would do the disciplinary trick here:

> Because he understood this the heroines of Saratchandra always fed the hero an extra mouthful of rice. The apparent simplicity of Saratchandra's and other similar writers' writing is actually very complex and to be thought of in the evening, peacefully after a glass of wood apple nectar. There is too much influence of fun and games in the lives of the people who traffic in studies and intellectualism in West Bengal and therefore they should stress the word apple correspondingly. We have no idea of the loss we are sustaining because we do not stress the wood apple-type herbal remedies correspondingly.

Speaking in code, then, we might say that to diagnose all Third World literature in English translation, by way of a sanctioned ignorance of the original, as a realism not yet graduated into language-games, is a species of 'stress upon the wood apple-type-herbal remedies correspondingly.' Such a minimalizing reading would docket Mahasweta's story as nothing more than a 'realistic' picture of Indian gendering.

In his account of the Subaltern Studies Conference (January 1986) where an earlier version of this paper was read, and where Mahasweta presented her own reading of 'Stanadayini,' David Hardiman comes to the following conclusion: '[Mahasweta's] down-to-earth style made for excellent theatre, with Gayatri being upstaged.'[84] I have obviously taken Mahasweta's reading, 'not unsurprisingly' as Hardiman writes, 'greatly at variance with Gayatri Spivak's,' seriously enough to engage with it in writing; and I have commented elsewhere on the implicit benevolent sexism of some subalternist work.[85] Yet I must point out that Hardiman's gesture is explicitly masculist: turning women into rivals by making them objects of the gaze. Beyond this particular male voyeurism, beyond the ontological/epistemological confusion that pits subaltern being against elite knowing, beyond the nativist's resistance to theory when it is recognizably different from her or his own unacknowledged theoretical position, I hope these pages have made clear that, in the *mise-en-scène* where the text persistently rehearses itself, writer and reader are both upstaged. If the teacher clandestinely carves out a piece of action by using the text as a tool, it is only in celebration of the text's apartness (*être-à-l'écart*). Paradoxically, this apartness makes the text susceptible to a history larger than that of the writer, reader, teacher. In that scene of writing, the authority of the author, however seductively down-to-earth, must be content to stand in the wings.

1987

Notes

1. A longer version of this essay appeared in Spivak, *In Other Worlds*, under a different title. Documentation has not been updated. This title and the general argument refers to an exchange between the author and translator for which please refer to Devi, ['In One Life'], *Proma* (serialized). Melanie Klein would have ironed out that difference.

2. Roland Barthes, 'The Reality-Effect,' in *The Rustle of Language*, tr. Richard Howard (New York: Hill and Wang, 1984).

3. The relationship between the two words that relate through this approximate differential is, of course, not 'the same' in all languages. There is, however, always a differential. In modern French and German, for example, the words for 'history' and 'story' being roughly the same, the manoeuvrings would be somewhat different from what we, writing in English, would argue. Ultimately the distinction is between the true and the sanctioned non-true.

4. Samik Bandyopadhyay, 'Introduction,' in Mahasweta Devi, *Five Plays: Mother of 1084/Aajir/Bayen/Urvashi and Johnny/Water* (Calcutta: Seagull Books, 1997).

5. Unpublished intervention, Subaltern Studies Conference, Calcutta, January 9, 1986.

6. 'The tenor is the gist of the thought concerning the subject [here India as Slave/Mother] . . . and the vehicle is that which embodies the tenor—the analogy [here the specificity of Jashoda as subaltern] . . . by which the tenor is conveyed' [Sylvan Barnet, et al., *A Dictionary of Literary, Dramatic and*

Cinematic Terms (second edition, Boston: Little, Brown, 1971)], p. 51.

7. This is the implicit grounding presupposition of Benedict Anderson, *Imagined Communities: Reflections on the Origin and Spread of Nationalism* (London: New Left Books, 1983). For a review expressing the criticism I here echo, see Ranajit Guha, 'Nationalism Reduced to "Official Nationalism",' *ASAA Review* 9, 1 (July 1985).

8. See Edward W. Said, *Culture and Imperialism* (London: Chatto & Windus, 1993).

9. See Partha Chatterjee, *Nationalist Thought and the Colonial World: A Derivative Discourse* (London: Zed Press, 1986). Uday Mehta, Assistant Professor of Government at Cornell University, is engaged in similar work on Lockean liberalism.

10. David Hardiman has examined some of the received wisdom on this issue in 'Bureaucratic Recruitment and Subordination in Colonial India: The Madras Constabulary, 1859–1947,' *Subaltern Studies*, vol. 4.

11. Hardiman, '"Subaltern Studies" at Crossroads,' *Economic and Political Weekly* (February 15, 1986).

12. *Mutatis mutandis.* Louis Althusser, 'Ideology and Ideological State Apparatuses (Notes Towards An Investigation),' *Lenin and Philosophy and Other Essays*, tr. Ben Brewster (New York: Monthly Review Press, 1971), still seems the most authoritative account of this phenomenon. Disciplinary productions such as historiography and literary pedagogy would probably fall between 'the educational' and 'the cultural ISA' –s (p.143).

13 See Terry Eagleton, 'The Rise of English,' *Literary Theory: An Introduction* (Minneapolis: University of Minnesota Press, 1983).

14. The most spirited discussion of the historicity of affects is to be found in the debate on pornography in the United States. For a discussion of the phenomenality of affects see

Robert C. Solomon, *The Passions* (Notre Dame: University of Notre Dame Press, 1976). For a provocative suggestion about Freud's contribution to the latter issue, see Derrida, *Of Grammatology*, tr. Spivak, p. 88.

15. I am, of course, describing deconstructive literary criticism when I cite these special themes. I take this position in spite of Derrida's cautionary words regarding the too positivistic use of 'themes' in an assessment of his own work ('The Double Session,' *Dissemination*, tr. Barbara Johnson [Chicago: University of Chicago Press, 1981], p. 245). In fact, in 'Varieties of Deconstructive Practice,' a widely publicized paper, I have distinguished Derrida's reading of literature from his reading of philosophical texts in terms of the issue of 'themes'. I mention this because that argument is also an issue of disciplinary production: of philosophy and literature, as here of history and literary pedagogy. For one of the most astute formulaic reductions of deconstruction to thematic reading, see Barbara Johnson, 'Teaching Deconstructively,' in G. Douglas Atkins and Michael L. Johnson, eds., *Writing and Reading Differently: Deconstruction and the Teaching of Composition and Literature* (Lawrence: University of Kansas Press, 1985). For an example of my own excursion into thematizing 'affirmative deconstruction,' see note 73 of this essay.

16. Quoted in Abiola Irele, *The African Experience in Literature and Ideology* (London: Heinemann, 1981), p. 1.

17. In the US, anti-economistic 'cultural' Marxism, feminist or androcentric, faults Althusser's work because it apparently underplays the class struggle by structuralizing the mode of production narrative. In Britain, the general impact of E. P. Thompson's critique, as reflected in *The Poverty of Theory and Other Essays* (London: Merlin, 1978) diagnosed Althusser as using Hegel as a code word for Stalin and betraying the spirit of Marxism by structuralizing the mode of production of narrative. On and around the issue of essentialism, a certain alliance between British post-Althusserianism and British Marxist feminism may be found. The work of Toril Moi in *Sexual/Textual Politics: Feminist Literary Theory* (New York:

Methuen, 1985) would be a good example.

18. Lise Vogel, *Marxism and the Oppression of Women: Toward a Unitary Theory* (New Brunswick: Rutgers University Press, 1983), p. 147.

19. Perry Anderson, *Passages from Antiquity to Feudalism* (London: New Left Books,1974), pp. 24–25.

20. Some-well known examples among many would be Mary O'Brien, *The Politics of Reproduction* (Boston: Routledge & Kegan Paul, 1981), Annette Kuhn and AnnMarie Wolpe, 'Feminism and Materialism,' in Kuhn and Wolpe, eds., *Feminism and Materialism: Women and Modes of Production* (London, 1978), and Rosalind Coward, *Patriarchal Precedents: Sexuality and Social Relations* (London: Methuen, 1983). See also Lydia Sargent, ed., *Women and Revolution* (Boston: South End Press, 1981).

21. Vogel, *Marxism and the Oppression of Women*, pp. 141–142. For a sound critique of the Engelsian-feminist position, see Coward, 'The Concept of the Family in Marxist Theory,' *Patriarchal Precedents*. It seems to me unfortunate that Coward's critique should be used to lead us back into Freud.

22. Karl Marx, *Capital*, tr. David Fernbach (New York: Vintage Books, 1978), vol. 2, pp. 469–471.

23. Ibid., pp. 180 and 180f. in general.

24. (Paris, 1980.)

25. V. N. Volosinov, *Marxism and the Philosophy of Language*, tr. Ladislav Matejka and I. R.Titunik (Cambridge: Harvard University Press, 1973), p. 68.

26. I am not arguing here for individual differences. On the social character of 'solitary self-experience,' see Volosinov, *Marxism and the Philosophy of Language*, pp. 89–94. In a more essentialist form, assuming that there is such a thing as 'life in its immediacy,' one might say, with Adorno: 'He [sic] who wishes to know the truth about life in its immediacy must scrutinise its estranged form, the objective powers that

determine individual existence even in its most hidden recesses' [Theodor Adorno, *Minima Moralia: Reflections from a Damaged Life,* tr. E. F. N. Jephcott (London: New Left Books, 1974), p. 15].Institutional subject-positions are social vacancies that are of course not filled in the same way by different individuals. All generalizations made from subject-positions are untotalizable.

27. See note 20 and, for the best-known examples, see Ann Oakley, *The Sociology of Housework* (New York: Pantheon, 1975), and the excellent documentation in Anne Ferguson, 'On Conceiving Motherhood and Sexuality: A Feminist Materialist Approach,' in Joyce Trebilcot, ed., *Mothering: Essays in Feminist Theory* (Totowa: Rowman & Allenheld, 1984), an essay I discuss below. Extended considerations might take their lead from the papers of the International Wages for Housework Campaign and check such sources as Gary S. Becker, *Human Capital: A Theoretical and Empirical Analysis with Special Reference to Education* (Chicago: University of Chicago Press, 1983).

28. For a discussion of feminist knowledge within existing paradigms, I have profited from listening to Susan Magarey, 'Transgressing Barriers, Centralising Margins, and Transcending Boundaries: Feminism as Politicised Knowledge,' paper presented at a conference on 'Feminist Enquiry As A Transdisciplinary Enterprise,' University of Adelaide, August 21, 1986.

29. Here I an invoking one of the earliest deconstructive positions: that reversals of positions legitimize each other and therefore a persistent effort at displacement is in order. For the later suggestion of a distancing from the project of reason, see Derrida, 'The Principle of Reason: the University in the Eyes of its Pupils,' *Diacritics* 13, 3 (Fall 1983).

30. Ferguson, 'Conceiving Motherhood,' p. 176.

31. In fact, Ferguson sees foster-mothering as one among many types of 'social mothering (adoptive mothers, step and foster mothers, older sisters, other mother surrogates)

[which] involves a second or different kind of mother-daughter bond' (p. 177). I discuss 'Stanadayini''s treatment of varieties of mother-child relationships later in the essay.

32. Ferguson, 'Conceiving Motherhood,' p.156.

33. This is to be distinguished from uninformed anti-Marxist positions. I have in mind generalizations in such powerful essays as Catharine A. McKinnon, 'Feminism, Marxism, Method, and the State: An Agenda for Theory,' in Nannerl O. Keohane, ed., *Feminist Theory: A Critique of Ideology* (Chicago: University of Chicago Press, 1982), Luce Irigaray, 'The Power of Discourse' and 'Commodities Among Themselves,' *This Sex Which Is Not One*, tr. Catherine Porter (Ithaca: Cornell University Press, 1985), pp. 82–85, 192–197, and Rosalind Coward, 'The Concept of the Family in Marxist Theory,' *Patriarchal Precedents.* It should be mentioned here that, in spite of her over-simplification of Marx's positions on value and ideology, Ferguson is generally politically astute in her assessment of the relationships between various domination systems in Euramerica.

34. Ferguson, 'Conceiving Motherhood,' p. 155.

35. Hannelore Mabry, 'The Feminist Theory of Surplus Value,' in Edith Hoshino Altbach et al. eds., *German Feminism: Readings in Politics and Literature* (Albany: State University of New York Press, 1986), tries interestingly to bridge the two spheres.

36. Anna Davin, 'Imperialism and Motherhood,' *History Workshop* 5 (1978).

37. Jenny Sharpe, *Allegories of Empire: The Figure of Woman in the Colonial Text* (Minneapolis: Univ. of Minnesota Press, 1993).

38. Ferguson, 'Conceiving Motherhood,' p. 175.

39. See Chandra Talpade Mohanty, 'Under Western Eyes: Feminist Scholarship and Colonial Discourses,' *boundary* 2 12, 3/13, 1 (Spring—Fall 1984) and 'Feminist Theory and the Production of Universal Sisterhood,' unpublished paper,

conference on 'Race, Culture, Class: Challenges to Feminism,' Hampshire College, December 1985, and Spivak, 'Imperialism and Sexual Difference,' *Oxford Litertary Review* 8, 1–2, 1986.

40. The discontinuities between the three domination systems are quietly revealed by the asymmetry in the articulation of the three pairs.

41. Antonio Gramsci, 'Some Aspects of the Southern Question,' *Selections from Political Writing: 1921–1926,* tr. Quintin Hoare (New York, 1978): Marx, *Capital,* tr. David Fernbach (New York, 1981), vol. 3, p. 1016.

42. Georg Wilhelm Friedrich Hegel, *Lectures on the Philosophy of History,* tr. J. Sibree (New York: Dover, 1956), p. 105, Adorno, *Mimima Moralia,* p. 53. Jurgen Habermas, 'A Philosophico-Political Profile,' *New Left Review* 151, Julia Kristeva, 'Memoires,' *L'infini* 1.

43. Meaghan Morris, 'Identity Anecdotes,' *Camera Obscura* 12 (1984), p. 43.

44. Davin, 'Imperialism,' p. 54.

45. Bharati Mukherjee, *Wife* (Boston: Houghton Mifflin, 1975) and *Darkness* (Markham, Ontario: Penguin, 1985).

46. Parvathy Hadley, 'The Betrayal of Superwoman,' *Committee on South Asian Women Bulletin* 4, 1 (1986), p. 18.

47. One of the pioneering statements, Zillah Eisenstein's 'Developing A Theory of Captialist Patriarchy and Socialist Feminism,' in Eisenstein, ed., *Captialist Patriarchy and the Case for Socialist Feminism* (New York, 1979), shows both the strengths and the weaknesses of this approach.

48. This is not in disagreement with the identification of rape with violence as in Catherine A. McKinnon, *Sexual Harassment of Working Women: A Case of Sex Discrimination* (New Haven: Yale University Press, 1979).

49. See Mahmoud Mamdani, *The Myth of Population Control:*

Family, Caste and Class in An Indian Village (New York: Monthly Review Press, 1973). For an unfortunate articulation of this contradiction, see Germaine Greer, *Sex and Destiny: the Politics of Human Fertility* (New York: Harper & Row, 1984).

50. For a use of the phrase in a single-issue class-context see 'Right to Life, but . . . ' *Economic and Political Weekly* 20.29 (July 20, 1985), editorial.

51. This is a general feeling that is too pervasive to document satisfactorily. But notice the interesting undertone emerging in 'French Texts/American Contexts,' *Yale French Studies* 62 (1981).

52. For representative pieces see Irigaray, 'When Our Lips Speak Together,' *This Sex*, Monique Wittig, *The Lesbian Body*, tr. David Le Vay (New York: Avon, 1975), Alice Schwarzer, 'The Function of Sexuality in the Oppression of Women,' in *German Feminism*, and Spivak, 'French Feminism in An International Frame,' *In Other Worlds*, pp. 134–153.

53. In *Feminine Sexuality: Jacques Lacan and the ecole freudienne*, tr. Juliet Mitchell and Jacqueline Rose (London: Routledge & Kegan Paul, 1982).

54. Lacan, 'Love Letter,' p. 159.

55. See, for examples, Hegel, *Aesthetics: Lectures on Fine Art*, tr. T. M. Knox (Oxford: Oxford University Press, 1975), Georg Lukacs. *Theory of the Novel*, tr. Anna Bostock (Cambridge: MIT Press, 1971), and Roland Barthes, *S/Z*, tr. Richard Miller (New York: Hill and Wang, 1974).

56. Jameson, *The Political Unconscious: Narrative As a Socially Symbolic Act* (Ithaca: Cornell University Press, 1981).

57. It is possible to deduce Althusser's reading of Lacan in this way. See Althusser, 'Freud and Lacan,' in *Lenin and Philosophy*.

58. Lacan, 'God and the Jouissance of the Woman,' in *Feminine Sexuality*, p. 142.

59. Derrida at once participates in and criticizes this gender-positioned definition of the object that cannot be known as the feminine thing when, in *Glas* (Paris: Galilée, 1981), he abbreviates the Hegelian Absolute Knowledge (*savoir absolu*), beyond the grasp of the individual subject, as *Sa.* In French this is a possessive pronominal article which merely indicates that its object is feminine.

60. For a discussion of use-value as theoretical fiction see Spivak, 'Speculation on Reading Marx: After Reading Derrida,' in Derek Attridge et al., eds., *Post-Structuralism and the Question of History* (Cambridge: Cambridge University Press, 1987), pp. 39–40.

61. 'Guiding Remarks for A Congress,' in *Feminine Sexuality*, p. 89.

62. For discussions of giving a face to the wholly Other, see Derrida, 'Violence and Metaphysics: An Essay on the Thought of Emmanuel Lévinas,' in *Writing and Difference*, tr. Alan Bass (Chicago, 1978), and Paul de Man, 'Autobiography As De-facement,' *The Rhetoric of Romanticism* (New York: Columbia University Press, 1984).

63. Subhas Bhattacharya, *Adhunik Banglar Prayog Abhidhan* (Calcutta: D. M. Library, 1984), p. 222.

64. Susan Sontag, *Illness As Metaphor* (New York: Random House, 1979).

65. Ibid., p. 43.

66. Lacan, 'Love Letter,' p. 159.

67. In 'Can the Subaltern Speak? Speculations on Widow-Sacrifice,' *Wedge* 7/8 (Winter/Spring 1985).

68. Franz Fanon's comments on 'Colonial War and Mental Disorders' are particularly pertinent here [*The Wretched of the Earth*, tr. Constance Farrington (New York:Grove Press, 1963)].

69. Lacan, 'Love Letter,' p. 160.

70. Spivak, 'Can the Subaltern Speak?' p. 123.

71. 'For the wish to sleep is the indeterminably significative tendency that is marking or repetition, and also the wish to forget about it, and to go on with the hypothesis that one is perceiving a meaningful form,' Cynthia Chase, 'The Witty Butcher's Wife: Freud, Lacan, and the Conversion of Resistance to Theory,' revised version, paper presented at a conference on 'Psychoanalysis and Feminism,' State University of Illinois, May 1–4, 1986.

72. Suggestion made at Subaltern Studies Conference, Calcutta, January, 1986. I believe it is a comparable impulse that prompts Derrida to place, in the right hand column of *Glas,* the torrential production of an unsystematizable slang in Jean Genet over against the definitive establishment of philosophical vocabulary in Hegel's work, treated in the left-hand column of the book. See also my treatment of 'rumour' in 'Subaltern Studies.'

73. Most rhetorical questions, such as the cook's 'What's there to tell?' imply a negative answer: 'Nothing.' Jashoda's story tells itself by (mis)understanding the question as literal and answering: 'this.'Such would be the morphology of 'affirmative deconstruction,' which says 'yes' to everything, not as a proper negation which leads to a strategically exclusive synthesis, but by way of an irreducible and originary 'mistake' that will not allow it to totalize its practice. This affirmation is not the 'yes' of pluralism or repressive tolerance, which is given from a position of power. 'Stanadayini' as *énonciation* might thus be an example of an ever-compromised affirmative deconstruction.

74. Kristeva, 'Ne dis rien,' *Tel Quel* 90 (1981). I am grateful to Cynthia Chase for having brought this essay to my attention.

75. Incidentally, her method here is conservative, in that she annuls what was most radical in Freud's hypothesis, namely infantile sexuality. ['In the hands of post-Freudians, helped no doubt by hesitations in Freud's own account, orthodox assumptions asserted themselves,' Jeffrey Weeks, 'Masculinity

and the Science of Desire,' *Oxford Literary Review* 8.1–2 (1986), p. 32.]. She positivizes and naturalizes into a psychic scenario the pre-originary space that is no more than an unavoidable methodological presupposition.

76. Kristeva is openly anti-Marxist. By aligning her work with Althusser's—'interpellation' is his notion of the subject's being 'hailed' in ideology ('Ideology and the State,' *Lenin and Philosophy*. pp. 170–77)—I am giving her the benefit of the doubt.

77. See Kristeva, 'Stabat mater,' in Susan Rubin Suleiman, ed., *The Female Body in Western Culture: Contemporary Perspectives* (Cambridge: Harvard University Press, 1986). Generalizing about femininity on the avowed basis of monotheism, and dismissing 'progressive activism' as versions of 'feminine psychosis,' this celebrated essay is a paean to motherhood sustained by thinly veiled autobiographical 'evidence' in the left-hand column and sweeping historico-psychoanalytic conclusions in the right about the 'virgin maternal' as coping with 'female paranoia' (pp. 116, 117, 114). With reference to Anne Ferguson's excellent essay, I had mentioned the sudden appearance of a 'cross-cultural referent' (see pages 16–17). These quick and often misleading definitive moments invoking an imaginary 'Third World' influence feminist thinking. In Eisenstein for example, the description of 'pre-capitalist society' where 'men, women, and children worked together in the home, the farm, or on the land to produce the goods necessary for their lives,' [and] women were procreators and child-rearers, but the organization of work limited the impact of this sexual role distinction' (*Capitalist Patriarchy*, p. 30), would be instantly corrected by the account of gendering within the heterogeneity of decolonized space offered by 'Stanadayini.' In Kristeva, the Blessed Virgin appropriates reincarnation in a flash: 'Mary does not die but rather—echoing Taoist and other oriental beliefs in which human bodies pass from one place to another in a never-ending flow [*flux*] which is in itself an imprint [*calque*] of the maternal receptacle [*réceptacle maternal*]—she passes over

[*transite*]' (Suleiman, *Female Body*, p. 105).

78. The question of the gaze has been most fully discussed in film theory. See for example, Laura Mulvey, 'Visual Pleasure and Narrative Cinema,' *Screen* 16.3 (1975), E. Ann Kaplan, *Women and Film: Both Sides of the Camera* (London: Methuen, 1983), Teresa de Lauretis, *Alice Doesn't: Feminism, Semiotics, Cinema* (Bloomington: Indiana University Press, 1984). See also Norman sBryson, *Vision and Painting: The Logic of the Gaze* (New Haven: Yale University Press, 1983). I am grateful to Frances Bartkowski for suggesting this book to me.

79. See Spivak, 'Displacement and the Discourse of Woman.'

80. In this connection, see Temma Kaplan's interesting notion of 'female consciousness' in 'Female Consciousness and Collective Action: the Case of Barcelona, 1910–1918,' in Keohane ed., *Feminist Theory.*

81. For two examples among many, consider Rabindranath Tagore, *Bhanusingher Padabali* (1291, Bengali year) and Bankimchandra Chattyopadhyaya, *Krishnacharitra* (1886).

82. I am grateful to Sudipto Kaviraj for having suggested to me that English is a medium of defilement in 'Stanadayini.'

83. It is immaterial to my point that there is an actual place by this name in Bengal.

84. Hardiman, 'Subaltern Studies,' p. 290.

85. Spivak, 'Subaltern Studies,' pp. 356–363.

behind the bodice:choli ke pichhe[1]

mahasweta devi

WHAT IS THERE was the national problem that year. When it became a *national issue*, the other fuckups of that time—e.g. crop failure-earthquake, everywhere clashes between socalled terrorists and statepower and therefore killings, the beheading of a young man and woman in Haryana for the crime of marrying out of caste, the unreasonable demands of Medha Patkar and others around the Narmada dam, hundreds of rape-murder-*lockup* torture et cetera *non-issues* which by natural law approached but failed to reach highlighting in the newspapers—all this remained *non-issues*.[2] Much more important than this was choli ke pichhe—behind the bodice.

That *issues* will and do trample upon *non-issues* in the life of the nation, this is the rule. This is why 'what is there' becomes so important. Proof that India's spirit is not only sealed in slumber, it can wake as needed.

Thus, everyone got busy to find out what was there: national *media, censor-board,* liberated anti-*bra* girls—many associations-organizations on the state-level etc. etc.—cable-tv *channels*—green eye*shaded lady votarians'* associations—all the religious groups—and politicians. Watching cassettes of *Khalnayak* under cover became the '*norm of the day.*'

Only upon seeing the *nation* busy with thoughts of this description did wellwishers create explosions in Bombay and Calcutta. In order to bring the nation's brain home—and thus India suddenly discovered that behind the bodice was the Middle East. This discovery was yet another explosion. Because the edifice crumbled was it suddenly known that it is the *Middle East* that controls the putting on and taking off of bodices and subsequent hankypanky etc. That *powerful lobby,* which is engaged in sending *messages* to the brain of the youthful generation to the effect that Bombay *films* are the cultural medium for representing Indian popular culture, that *lobby* was pissed off at this. The leader (honorary and pleased if able to attend *seminars*) of their *counterlobby* (exceedingly sparsely peopled) prints a *handbill* that enters the fold of each newspaper and declares that each year, behind the length of the *raw stock footage* of Bombay *films,* which can circle the globe in a foolproof slipknot, is a similar nation state that makes the Indian masses laugh, weep, dance, and sing by remote control, etc. etc. Reading this news mad Haripada climbs to the roof of the Tata *Building* and shouts '*Invasion! Invasion!*' and is swiftly thrown in jail by way of the ATADF *Act* (*Anti-Terroristic and Disruptive Forces Act*).[3] Which prison, who imprisoned him, this is not known. The word '*invasion*' worries the nation. The 106-year old freedom fighter Gopikrishnababu says, Eh, is the English coming to take India again by *invading* it, eh?—Now from the entire country, Indian intellectuals not knowing a single Indian language meet in a closed *seminar* in the capital city and make the following wise decision known. *Cultural invasion* is much more dangerous than *cultural revolution.* So India is doing what India must do to hold it back. There is no Russia. Marx-Lenin-Mao-Zedong have failed. The natural vacuum must be filled with *pirated cassettes.* In that sense 'Behind the Bodice' or Choli ke Pichhe is an elixir for the times. After all this Shaili's Mother wraps her huge and ever-enlarging corpus in just one piece of cloth and goes on saying, 'Never dragged on a *belouse* [blouse] in my life, how to put on a choli now!'[4] Because the *nation* was busy with all this Upin's news got only an inch-and-a-half of space in the newspaper. Escaped the nation's eye.

2

Upin's news did not appear in the paper as news of Upin. It was also not known at first that a nameless person's corpse crushed by the wheels of a railway train midway between Jharoa and Seopura was Upin's body. Already before that Upin's friend and sidekick Ujan had received a *postcard, Come to Jharoa. Very urgent*—Upin. This is the letter that took Ujan to Jharoa to find out Upin's end. The postcard had given Ujan a great shock.

Now he remembers the first phase of Upin's becoming a missing person. Naturally he took the letter to Shital Mallya. A dead end road in the Salt Lake area of Calcutta, large trees to its south and then the everflowing Keshtopur canal—to the north a few extraordinary houses—Shital had come there to her own apartment. Why such a beautiful, firm and fit, youthful at thirty-three body is called Shital or Cold, Ujan doesn't know. Upin and Shital are husband and wife—but Upin is an itinerant ace-photographer, Shital a famous Himalaya-climber—the two don't spend even a month and a half out of the year together—yet how they remain in love with each other, this too Ujan doesn't know. Ujan can remain greatly unknowing. Ujan is devoted to Upin alone. From time to time Upin goes to Bihar and Orissa to take photos, and he takes Ujan. Since Upin's pictures go at *top* rates abroad and at home, Ujan benefits as well. The apartment in Salt Lake is not to Ujan's tastes. No one lives there, in an impossibly impeccable apartment. Once in a while Shital comes, everything seems problematic. Of course Upin says, Why think about it? Shital is a child of Nature. This dead end road, this green—this silent narrow canal, these she needs.

Shital is supposed to be two people. Violent and *aggressive* Shital attacks the Himalayas again and again. Calm, soft Shital sits submerged in this water-tree-silence. There is a great deal of natural beauty in India apart from the Himalayas and Salt Lake. Shital cannot bear those *landscapes.* Temperamentally Shital is a girl of 2094, or rather Shital's century has not yet come.

Upin says these things with a roaring laugh. You can't tell if Upin is thirty-five or fifty-five. He is of squarish build, bearded, with too-bright eyes. He takes a bath once every few days, eats meat and drinks beer, smokes country cigarettes, in the corner room of Ujan's home, subdivided among the branches of the extended family. In a pricey Delhi hotel he is equally *at home*—an *Esperanto* man.

Now Shital sat still, looking at the flowing canal.

Ujan gives Shital the *postcard*.

Oh, Jharoa.

So he writes.

Not to me.

But you are usually in Kadamkuri at this time.

But he went to Delhi also from Jharoa.

Yes.

I told you to stick to him. You know how much work there is at the *apple-estate* at this time! I gave you money . . .

I would have looked after Upinda[5] even if you hadn't given me money! How could I know that he'd act so crazy in Delhi? I went to buy bidis, and the police . . .

Ujan's voice broke.

Yes. . . pictures in the papers . . . scandal! scandal!

Yes, the picture of a banner. Written on it in English, 'The halfnaked amplebreasted female figures of Orissa are about to be raped. *Save them! Save the breast!*'

I'd not been to Delhi before. Knew nothing of the city. I came back nonplussed finally.

Great!

Suddenly Ujan rashly says, I knew it was me he would inform. And so he did. I was, yes, waiting after I came back.

You didn't do too much.

Shital controls herself by deep breathing when she is angry or excited. She calms herself in a minute and says, *Why* Jharoa, Ujan?

You do know!

I only don't know why he went last time. Yes—elephants were migrating that time—

Then drought—

Then *pesticide* in the river water—

Famine conditions, *semifamine condition*—

Yes, yes, yes! All those pictures appeared in the *national press.* Also in *Lens Magazine.* That makes four times. And the fifth time?

Ujan is silent.

The fifth time?

I don't know. I went off to Bitala . . . Upinda didn't go.

Whose photos are these?

A highbreasted rural woman sits slack with her breast shoved into an infant's mouth. The breast is covered with the end of her cloth. The same girl is walking with many girls carrying water on her head. Breasts overflowing like full pitchers.

Whose photo, Ujan?

Ujan says, Gangor. Gangor what . . . that I don't know.

Shital is quite startled. Gangor? *You mean* Gangor? Gangauri?[6]

Meaning?

You are a *free-lance columnist,* Ujan! Don't names make you curious?

No. What's in a name?

Shital instantly becomes the erstwhile Shital Mallya, 'the *docu-maker* for the Festival of India.' Says in the voice that offers a *running commentary*, the Gangor festival takes place in Rajasthan, Ganga worship, Goddess Ganga. Strange! The Ganga River does not run through Rajasthan. Even large rivers . . .

The land of kings [literal meaning of 'Rajasthan'], perhaps there was Ganga once.

Sujan! Oh no, Ujan! You are *divine*! So little *cultural awareness*! Upin also says, Bengalis are *divine*! They don't think they need to know anything about the other states of India.

Where did you get these pictures?

Upin hid them. With Gangor, did Upin . . . ?

No.

Semifamine condition . . . Gangor's crowd came to Jharoa looking for work. They'll work on a piece wage basis in the kilns for light bricks and tiles. When Upin and Ujan arrived, they had already lived there for two or three months. Gangor's health was fine . . . Upin took a photo when he saw the baby suckling—Gangor did not object. But she put out her hand . . . money, Sir, rupees? Snap a photo so give me cash! Ujan got a *shock*. Upin crumpled up all the money in his pocket and gave it to her.

Walking towards the *PWD* [Public Works Department] bungalow Ujan had said, You gave her sixty-seventy rupees? What a shameless girl!

Upin had said, *Now now* Ujan! You found this *shocking*? Listen friend, I will sell these pictures . . . why shouldn't she take money? They are not dumb beasts Ujan, they understand, that even when the gentlemen distribute relief, they have some hidden agenda.

And then he'd said, God, those breasts are *statuesque*! Did you see the *mammal* projections?

I didn't look.

Happens, this happens. The uncle of a friend of mine went to Dandakaranya Forest after Independence. *Anthropologist.* Seeing the uncovered chests of Aboriginal women . . .

Shame on him.

He too said shame shame, and asked them to wear blouses. Now they do. Then they didn't. The man lost his mind little by little.

Leave it, talk about something else.

When I saw her breasts . . .

Shame Upinda! Aren't you married?

Learn to praise and respect a beautiful thing.

Gangor enters Upin's head. No, those pictures are not here. Gangor at night, roasting doughballs on a dried cowdung fire, bent slightly forward. Under the dirty red cloth the cleavage of her Konarak chest, resplendent.[7]

A train passing, Gangor's crowd looking at it. Her breasts like the cave paintings of Ajanta, against the backdrop of the sky.[8] Dirty choli. Dirty red cloth, hair full of lice, filth . . . filth . . .

The second time Gangor had said, Hundred rupees per picture.

Upin took off his watch and gave it to her.

Gangor threw away the watch. It was eleven ten. The watch stopped.

The watch is stopped, will remain so. Upin did not get the watch repaired.

Gangor shouted obscenities at the thunderstruck Upin. You bastard ball-less crook! Give me a watch with one hand, and tell the police I stole it? Go, go, old jerk.

Gangor's man came and took her away with a couple of slaps.

That very day Upin went and sat at the chullu [country liquor distilled with cheap chemicals]-stand. No, he cannot forget those *mammal projections.* It has become a seismic upheaval in his brain. Ujan! *There lies all the mystery.* How can this be?

Ujan was sitting on a sack of packed cement at a distance, there to fetch Upin.

He was very angry with Gangor then.

And it was to him that Gangor came.

Sir! Sir! He is not my man! Our contractor, he's come to make us work. My man . . . not in my room, Sir . . . the police beat him up for he steals . . . it's a bad place where I come from Sir.

Ujan said, Get out! Go!

Gangor was weeping and keening, with her cloth in her mouth. . . . Tell the camera-Sir, why not take me away? A cloth to wear . . . a bite to eat . . . a place to sleep for mother and child. . . . What to do Sir . . . no field, no land, living is very hard . . . pots and pans . . . stove and knife . . . cleaning rooms . . . laundry . . . I'll do anything Sir . . . [9]

> You have a husband!
>
> He can't come to my room Sir . . . comes under cover at night . . . I give him money . . . the contractors are not good people . . .
>
> Go away. I'll call the police otherwise.

Ujan walks off at speed. Real problem dragging Upin off. He kept saying, Gangor! Gangor! He and Ujan left the next day.

Upin was stony silent. Won't keep it . . . can't keep it,

Ujan . . . can't keep such a *bodyline* . . . not a thing will remain—do you realize that the breasts of the girls at Elora are eroding?[10] Gangor is *fantastic*!

Ujan!

Yes, Shital, tell me!

Is Upin . . .

Ujan came back to Calcutta. Said, no. Upinda says again and again, *Country liquor okay*! *Country women repel me*!

Shital smiled slightly.

You know no more about this girl?

No. And I don't want to know.

All right, what happened before going to Delhi?

Doesn't know, Ujan doesn't know. That Upin didn't go to Arunachal, but came to Calcutta, that too he doesn't know.

Didn't go to Arunachal. Came to Calcutta, I didn't know. Went to Jharoa, that too I didn't know. Suddenly he came to me in a great rush—hurtay-phurtay . . .

What?

Typical Bengali expression.

Don't be so typical. I don't understand Bengali all that well. What I learnt was for Upin! *Of course,* many of the mountaineers in our club are *Bengalis.* Upin's Bengali was altogether . . .

Punjabi only in name. Three generations in Calcutta.

Upin left Calcutta at eighteen.

He'd talk about it.

Then?

It seemed as if something dreadful had happened. He said, I've been running around a lot these last days . . .

Upin had said, O *hell*! I walked, got on *trucks*, travelled by police *jeep*—no trace of Gangor's group. No one says anything about where they are. The guard at the *bungalow* said, she has to come to Jharoa . . . Gangor has done something really bad . . . I got no info. A *conspiracy of silence*!

What would you have done with the information, Upinda? Ujan had said.

Would have brought her back.

Where?

Wherever.

For what?

You won't understand Ujan . . . I'd have saved her.

A *married* female.

Would I have . . . No, Ujan, no. I'm going to sleep.

Your *bags*?

I'm going to sleep.

You do know, Shital. He slept for three or four days—and then he said, I'll go to Delhi. *And* . . .

What will you do now?

Why, go to Jharoa. Won't you?

No. I'll wait for him.

Where?

In Kadamkuri!

Then I'll be off.

Yes.

Shouldn't you be going? You're the wife . . .

No. Our relationship is not like that at all. Upin gets lost. Comes back again. He and the *camera*—the Himalayas and I—perhaps in some distant future . . .

You will live in Kadamkuri?

Perhaps.

If you at least lived together. Such a human being . . . got crazed living constantly alone.

Where did you find him crazy?

Is *save the breast* not a craziness?

Upin no doubt doesn't think so. All right Ujan! Keep this cash. Phone me straightaway if you get him.

I don't need money.

Shital looked at the pictures with care. Chest, *breast.* What is the breast? *Fat tissue*, this that, a lot of bother.

Why was Upin so worried?

Ujan was leaving, he left. Shital closed the door and put her hand on her liquid silicone implanted front. Behind Shital's choli is a silicone chest. Upin had said, This is all artificial, Shital?

How would Upin know their secret—these breasts remain aggressive forever. Like plastic flowers, Shital? Upin would say.

'Had said'—'would say'—no, no, Upin has not become 'was,' for sure. Shital breathed deeply. Mind, be calm, be calm. Let Upin take all his pictures, let Shital's Himalaya-ascent come to an end, perhaps one will settle permanently in Kadamkuri some day.

Sujan Kabir entered the room. The pictures are still scattered. He took a look and said, Why is Upin so occupied with what's behind the choli?

Shital cannot answer. Ujan doesn't take the money.

3

Why Gangor and her natural, most complex sweat glands or bosom had turned Upin's head he didn't know.

The breast can be called a complex sweat gland. There is plenty of fat in it. This glandular collective is most charming. There are seventeen lactative *units*. The glands go to the stem of the breast. At childbirth the body's blood is transformed into milk.

Upin knew all this, he knew. Not a breast blessed by liquid silicone, but natural, hence unique. He felt that Gangor and her chest were endangered.

He was supposed to go to Arunachal before he went to Delhi, on the way the idea was born that his *destination* was Jharoa. Getting off at Calcutta and rushing helter skelter by *train* to Gomo—then *bus*—in such ways to Seopura. Then by train, getting off at Madhpura Halt, to Jharoa.

But even in the midday sun everyone was remaining silent in Jharoa, as if night had fallen. Nights are silent in Jharoa, days soundwaved. Now the days are silent too. Around the shacks and huts of Gangor's group, around the tile-roofed warehouses, their clothes were not drying on the lantana shrubs—no hubbub by the wellside.

Where, where, where?

The Watchman said, Shall I bring you some tea from the shop?

Where is Gangor's crowd?

Would you like to wash?

Where are they?

The contractor is wandering in the market area,

adrift. He doesn't know, none of the shop- or stall-keepers knows.

Upin went to Heshegora, to Lamdi, from village to village. In Lamdi in the afternoon Gangor's chullu-befuddled husband had spat on the ground on hearing 'Gangor.'

Hopeless, hopeless. Upin heard a child weeping. A skinny dark twelvish-year old girl was standing with a year-old boy on her hip. The boy was crying.

Suddenly a message flashes through Upin's brain. Upin realizes the boy must be Gangor's. And somewhere a terrible conspiracy is at work. That's why the people are stony silent.

The Caretaker had said, She has to come to Jharoa. Gangor has done a very bad thing.

The police were about in Jharoa.

Upin came back. Something fearful has happened somewhere. The *nation* doesn't know it. The earth shook in Upin's head, the ground cracked, the fault line belched out hot sand, closed, and cracked again, Ujan! Upin grasped, as the train went juddering on, that he would have to come to Jharoa again.

4

When Upin got there, Jharoa had broken its vow of silence. Upin felt it was his first arrival. The same shops, the same unspeakable chips-and-fried-sweets stalls engorged with the dust of buswheels. On this market day the cattle exchange worked as usual. But in his mind's core Upin sensed for sure, Gangor was there, right there. The Caretaker took a look at him, scowling. Somewhere 'choli ke pichhe' was playing.

You left your bag behind last time?

Have you kept the bag?

In my room. Where did you go looking and looking for Gangor?

Where is she?

She . . .

The Caretaker goes on, You ruined her with your pictures Sir, otherwise how would she dare?

What has Gangor done? Is she dead?

The Gangors of this world don't come to die Sir, they come to kill. Shameless country girl . . . jiggling her body all the time . . . saying to the market people, didn't snap your *photos*, snapped mine. See!

Then?

Gangor made everyone sin against God.

How?

She pressed charges against the police. When you came she was in Seopura.

Why?

Why not Sir? The jail is in Seopura, the big police station, the Courthouse. Isn't Seopura the county seat? It's there that she has to go now.

She's in Seopura now?

Where else? Come and go, come and go every week—the police is so tight on her back that even the contractors' *labour* has stopped coming Sir! Women have to be careful in Shiva's world.[11] You're punished if you don't understand this. The police came here because of the girl so many times . . . so many times . . . when the girl doesn't understand the police are men too, they will craze if you tease them.

Why, why, why will they go crazy?

She will smear the police, and the police will let her go? Have they ever? She could have run off on the *terain* [train] . . . but she pressed charges . . . she has to show up, and the police will . . .

Where is Gangor? And where is her child?

. . . and someone's wife at that!

Where is she, in the village?

Will anyone let her come into the village? No place there, no one talks to her in Jharoa—she comes from Seopura, and she does what is expected.

Where is she?

You'll see her in the market after dark. Drinking so much liquor . . .

Gangor drinks chullu?

What else?

I will take her away.

Nonsense Sir. You have a name, you're worth something. Who knew Jharoa? You took photos many times. You put us in the news—you'll take her?

She must be saved.

Upin's head wasn't working, he couldn't grasp what the Caretaker was saying.

But the police.

What can the Seopura police do? I've taken a lot of depositions from the Bihar police.[12] I'll put pictures in the news.

Come, take your bag, check it out. The police would have nicked it. You wash up. I'll get food from the *hotel.* She won't come before early evening.

Upin doesn't wash, he lies down on the *camp* bed. Sleeps till early evening. Ujan would have forced him to eat. Would have said you're going for days on *nervous energy*, you'll *collapse.*

Ujan, Upin has been *collapsing* for some time. Upin is a *failure.* What was the good of taking so many pictures of Jharoa, on so many different trips? So many died drinking poisoned water, so many *migrated* on account of crop failure—at that time Upin, aka the State Government—no, you can't call this famine. After all you see skeletal cattle at the market, food stinking of dust and diesel—*very busy video palace, very loud* 'choli ke pichhe', the national anthem of these times—Gangor knows what's behind it. And nothing has changed. There are more warehouses. A new police station, they harass the women. Obscene laughter, and they eat free food from the stalls. It's not for nothing that Upin is *collapsing.* Now Upin suffocates when he enters Shital's germfree dwelling. No, life must be re-cast from the beginning.

Upin woke up at dusk. Somewhere a feeling of vulnerability, for some time now an *obsession* has been spinning him like a top. Suddenly he feels he's alone in a place like this—he's alone everywhere. To live in such solitude, to have denied the natural demands of life so much, was perhaps not right. Gangor's developed breasts are natural, not manufactured. Why did he first think they were the object of photography? Why did it seem that that chest was endangered?—What is this craziness, Sir, go away, don't you have a home? The Caretaker has a home, wife and kids. There is no roof waiting for Upin, matrimony of arrangement—the sort of marriage that one sees everywhere. But now he must rescue Gangor. His sense of emergency takes him to the chullu stand, where it smells of curried tripes, of the strong country liquor, of halitosis, of the ordure that bubbles up in the open drain's thick scum, of the flushless shithole beyond the drain. Upin stops his nose, his ears, and sits down. Suddenly 'choli ke pichhe' starts playing.

And Gangor comes just then. Now she wears a red and yellow polyester cloth, smelling of stale dirt, and still—Upin lifts his eyes nervously—a very dark choli, very insolent breasts, oiled and braided hair, darting suspicious glance.

Upin and Gangor look at each other. A sharp experienced smile blooms on Gangor's lips. She pushes away some man's hands. Says, the Camera-Sir has been going around for me for a long time, Contractor. Today he's my client, eh Sir?

Upin offers himself, lets himself go.

Contractor, Gangor?

What to do, Sir? He knows nothing but contracting. But Bhusan! I've *pomoted* [promoted] you after all? It's all profit in this trade.

Everyone laughs, everyone. One says, Gangor, what's behind your bodice, love?

Come on Sir.

Gangor gets up. As if she says to Upin with her beckoning finger, Get thee behind me!

Then the broken road, the lantana shrubs, the railway tracks are all spread out, a broken bus is parked on a *siding*, now everything is up for sale, a working bus, as well as the broken down 'Mahavir.'[13] After that come rows of decrepit warehouses, Gangor walks fast. She kicks the tin door of a shack.

Upin can't see what else there is in the room. Gangor raises the wick and utters her own *running commentary* to herself.

There is more money in it if she goes to Seopura. But the police station will not let Gangor enter. She will have to remain in Jharoa and go to Seopura—the *date* for her *case* will come up, the police will take the *date.* Not enough money comes in that Gangor will run off somewhere. And where will she run—everyone now knows that Gangor identified them, had talked at the police station, had pointed them out, and that's how all was lost.

> Gangor!
>
> You snapped many many times my chest, Sir. But I knew your plan. Otherwise would you have given so much cash?
>
> Gangor!
>
> Will Gangor unwind her cloth, or just lift it? Do your stuff, twenty rupees. Spend the night, fifty, tell me quick.
>
> You are doing whore work, Gangor?
>
> What's it to you, son of a whore?
>
> You . . . take off . . . your blouse . . .

Gangor breathes hard. Says in a voice ragged with anger, Don't you hear? Constantly playing it, singing it, setting the boys on me . . . behind the bodice . . . the bodice . . . choli ke pichhe . . . choli ke . . .

> No Gangor . . .
>
> You are a bastard too sir . . . you took *photoks* [photos] of my chest, eh? OK . . . I'll show . . . but I'll take everything from your *pocket,* a - ll . . .

In the *silhouette* cast by the hurricane lantern two shadows act *violently.* Gangor takes off her choli and throws it at Upin. Look, look; look, straw—chaff, rags—look what's there.[14]

No breasts. Two dry scars, wrinkled skin, quite flat. The two raging volcanic craters spew liquid lava at Upin —*gang rape* . . . biting and tearing *gang rape* . . . *police* . . . a court *case* . . . again a *gang rape* in the *lockup* . . . now from Jharoa to Seopura . . . Seopura to Jharoa . . . the Contractor catches clients . . . terrorizes a *public* . . . plays the song, the song . . .

Upin stands up weaving, unsteady.

Gangor puts her hands in his *pockets* with skilled ease, scrabbles in his *pants pockets,* what a smell of violent resentment in her body . . . and then she kicks the ground.

Upin comes out, Gangor is still screaming, talking, kicking the *corrugated tin* walls with abandon. Upin runs. There is no *non-issue* behind the bodice, there is a rape of the people behind it, Upin would have known if he had wanted to, could have known.

Upin runs along the tracks.

5

Ujan got there much later. Jharoa was calm. A new *bus* station where the warehouses used to be. A new police station in Jharoa. He got a months-old picture of a dead man.

No one by the name of Gangor lived in Jharoa.

On paper the search for the missing Upin Puri is still active. But those kinds of *files* sink, way under other *files.*

1996

Notes

1. Title of a popular song in the Hindi film *Khalnayak*—'Villain' (1993). It means 'behind the bodice.' The first sentence of the story takes off from the first line of the song: Choli ke pichhe kya hai? What is behind the bodice? The answer is, of course, 'breasts.'

2. Once again, I italicize the words in English in the original. Because this makes the page difficult to read I reprint here a note from Devi, *Imaginary Maps* (New York edition: Routledge, 1995), Translator's Note.

> All words in English in the original have been italicized. This makes the English page difficult to read. The difficulty is a reminder of the intimacy of the colonial encounter. Mahasweta's stories are *post*colonial. They must operate *with* the resources of a History shaped by colonization *against* the legacy of colonialism. The language of the practical everyday life of all classes (including the subaltern), profoundly marked by English,mimes the historical sedimentation of colonialism by the degree to which the words and phrases have been lexicalized, and the degree to which, therefore, they exist 'independently' in Bengali. By contrast, the culturalist intellectual and the State can affect a 'pure' idiom, which disguises *neo*colonialist collaboration. (Since Bengali is not the national language of India, state interference is less noticeable. For that, one must turn to neighbouring Bangladesh—whose national language *is* Bengali—or to Hindi, which is the national language of India.)

Medha Patkar is an activist who mobilized the Aboriginals about to be displaced by the World Bank's Narmada Valley Project. Her argument was that a watery grave—*jalsamadhi*—was preferable to enforced nomadism, since rehabilitation invariably fell ridiculously short of its promise.

3. An imaginary version of the actual TADA (Terrorism and

Disruptive Activities) Act.

4. Shaili's Mother is making a distinction between 'blouse,' the more conservative top, covering the midriff, generally introduced by colonial influence; and the more 'ethnic,' bare-midriffed garment which became generally popular in the middle class in the fifties. 'Bodice,' in the English of Bengal, means a homemade undergarment. I am using the word in its international currency. The appellation '—'s Mother' is given by the Bengali middle class to domestic servants and is more generally used in the underclass.

5. 'Da' is a suffix added to the first name of an older man of the same generation and is a contraction of 'dada,' older brother.

6. The possible classical Sanskrit version of the peasant name Gangor. In the refined version, it would mean, roughly 'the Durga of the people,' or, even 'the fair-skinned woman of the people.' Note the relationship with Dopdi in 'Draupadi,' the Pandava queen with five husbands in the *Mahabharata.* The running commentary offered by Shital has rather little to do with the name suggested. Perhaps this relates to the documentation of 'ethnic' India being in the hands of intellectuals who know no Indian language? A more textual connection with 'ganadharshan' or 'the rape of the people' is discussed in the introductory essay.

7. Konarak: 13th-century erotic temple sculpture in Orissa.

8. 2nd century B. C.—6th century A. D. These sculptural examples are international and national tourist spots.

9. Here and subsequently, Gangor's speech is an untranslatable hybrid Dalit Hindi-Bengali which Mahasweta is among the very few Bengali writers to attempt in a sustained way.

10. Elora: Companion caves of Ajanta, between 5th century and 8th century A. D. (see note 8).

11. The God Shiva is, of course, Master of creation, preservation, and destruction in the high Hindu pantheon. But these people are undoubtedly a Shiva-worshipping sect, and therefore Shiva is their chief god.

12. Seopura is a village in the state of Bihar. Upin is thus putting the state police above the local force.

13. Common Indian habit of giving to privately owned public buses names from the epics. This word means the "man of great strength," but is also the appellation of the Monkey-god, devoted companion of Rama.

14. English cannot grasp the fall from the most respectful form of address—due to Upin's class from Gangor's—to the least.